Disney

Minnie & Daisy

Best Friends Forever

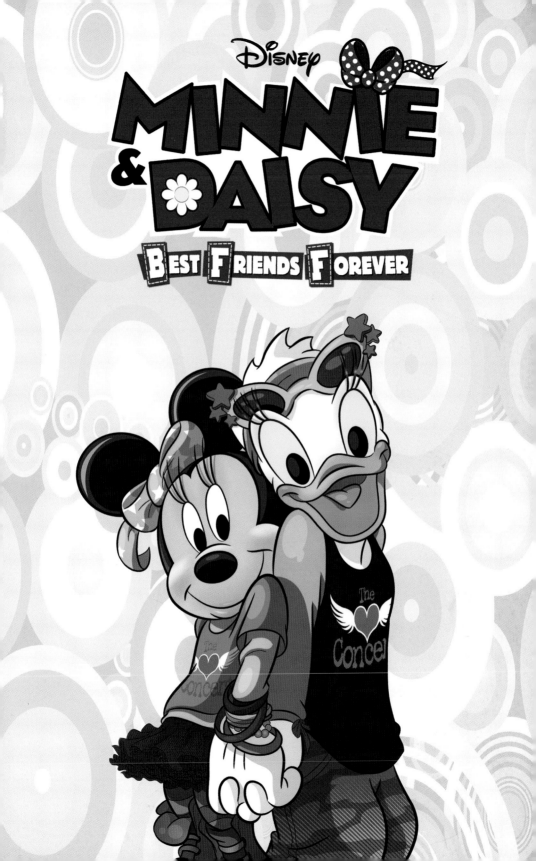

DISNEY FAIRIES

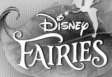

Graphic Novels Available from PAPERCUTZ

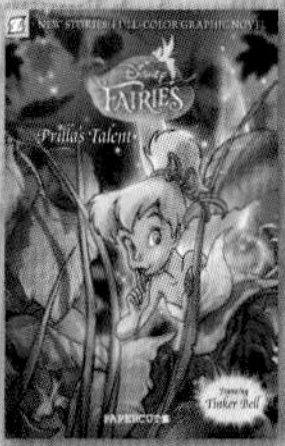

Graphic Novel #1
"Prilla's Talent"

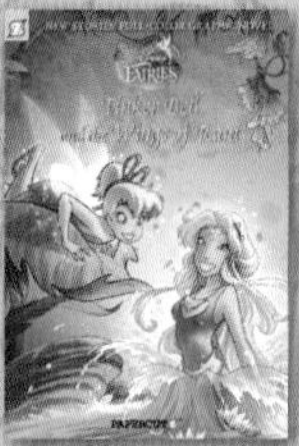

Graphic Novel #2
"Tinker Bell and the Wings of Rani"

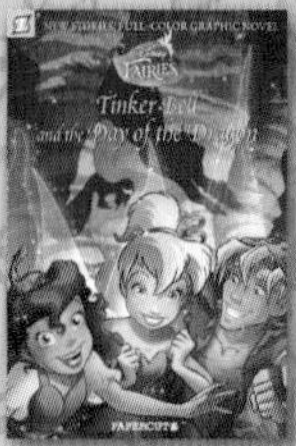

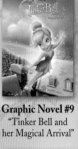

Graphic Novel #3
"Tinker Bell and the Day of the Dragon"

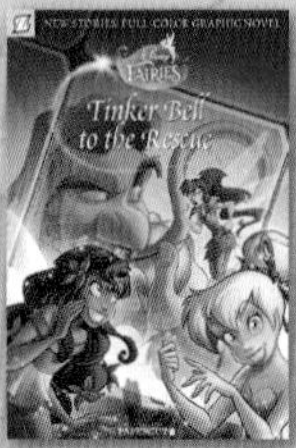

Graphic Novel #4
"Tinker Bell to the Rescue"

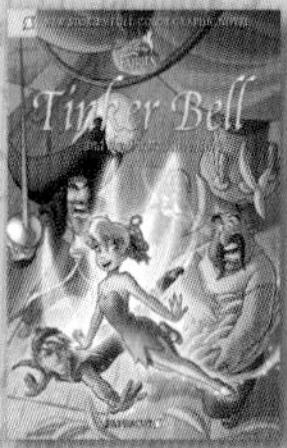

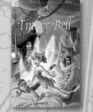

Graphic Novel #5
"Tinker Bell and the Pirate Adventure"

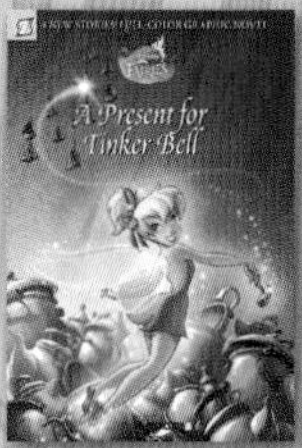

Graphic Novel #6
"A Present for Tinker Bell"

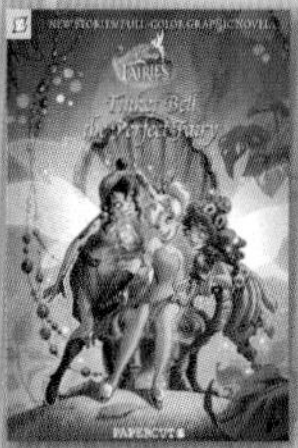

Graphic Novel #7
"Tinker Bell the Perfect Fairy"

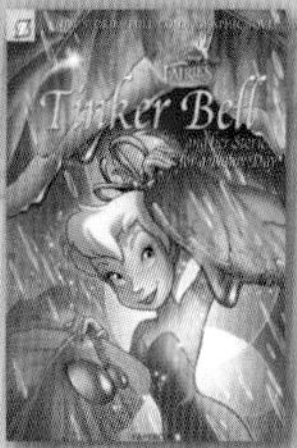

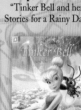

Graphic Novel #8
"Tinker Bell and her Stories for a Rainy Day"

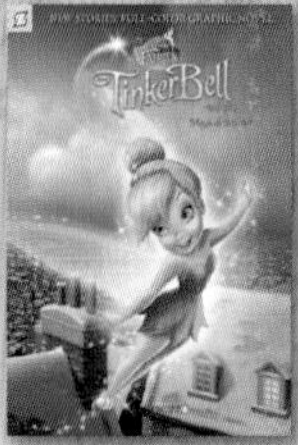

Graphic Novel #9
"Tinker Bell and her Magical Arrival"

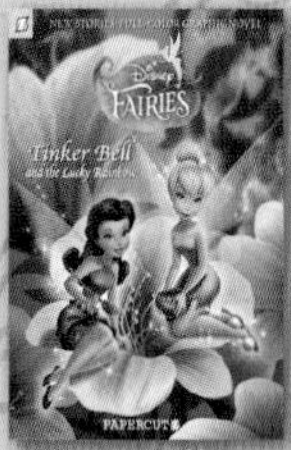

Graphic Novel #10
"Tinker Bell and the Lucky Rainbow"

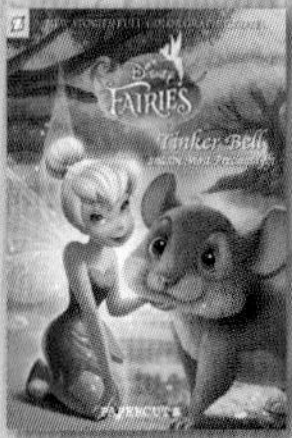

Graphic Novel #11
"Tinker Bell and the Most Precious Gift"

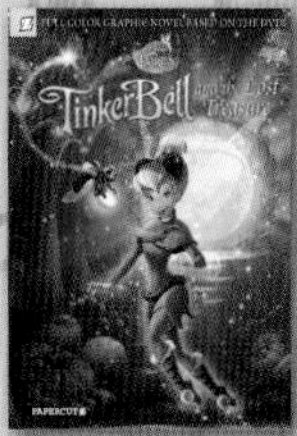

Graphic Novel #12
"Tinker Bell and the Lost Treasure"

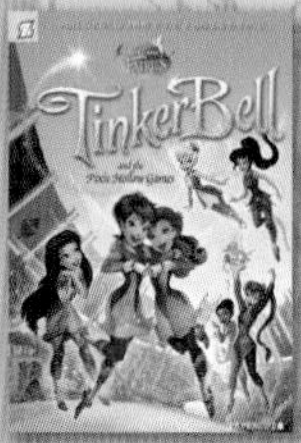

Graphic Novel #13
"Tinker Bell and the Pixie Hollow Games"

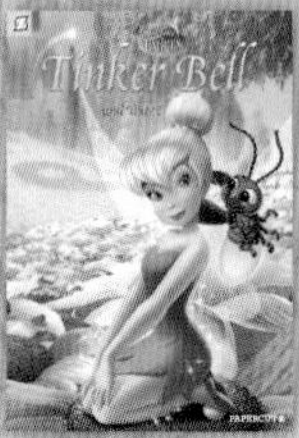

Graphic Novel #14
"Tinker Bell and Blaze"

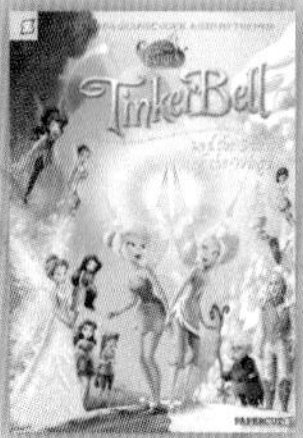

Graphic Novel #15
"Tinker Bell and the Secret of the Wings"

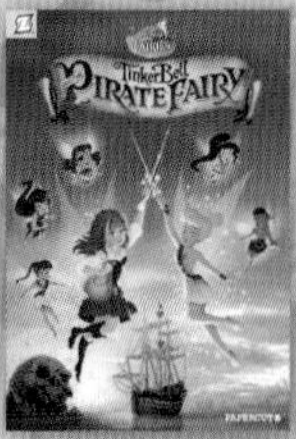

Graphic Novel #16
"Tinker Bell and the Pirate Fairy"

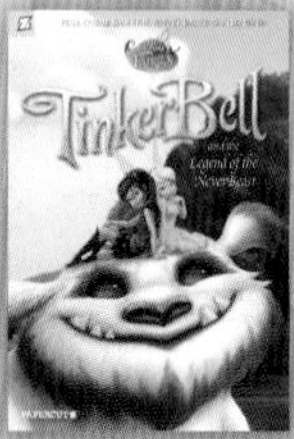

Graphic Novel #17
"Tinker Bell and the Legend of the NeverBeast"

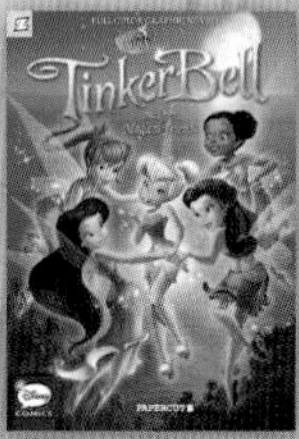

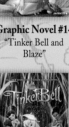

Graphic Novel #18
"Tinker Bell and her Magical Friends"

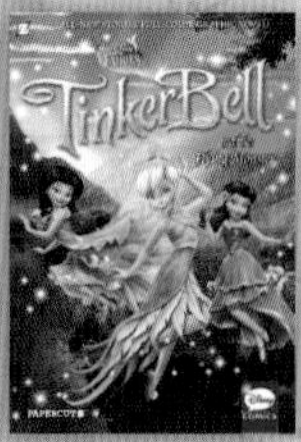

Graphic Novel #19
"Tinker Bell and the Flying Monster"

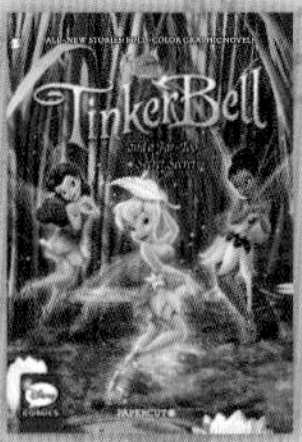

Graphic Novel #20
"Tinker Bell and a Far-Too-Secret Secret"

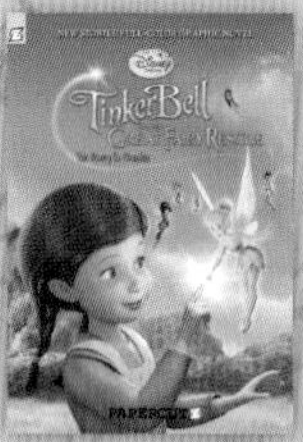

Tinker Bell and the Great Fairy Rescue

DISNEY FAIRIES graphic novels are available in paperback for $7.99 each; in hardcover for $12.99 each except #5, $6.99PB, $10.99HC, #6-14 are $7.99PB $11.99HC. Tinker Bell and the Great Fairy Rescue is $9.99 in hardcover only.
Available at booksellers everywhere.

See more at papercutz.com

Or you can order from us: Please add $4.00 for postage and handling for first book, and add $1.00 for each additional book. Please make check payable to NBM Publishing. Send to: Papercutz, 160 Broadway, Suite 700, East Wing, New York, NY 10038 or call 800 886 1223 (9-6 EST M-F) MC-Visa-Amex accepted.

Disney

Minnie & Daisy

Best Friends Forever

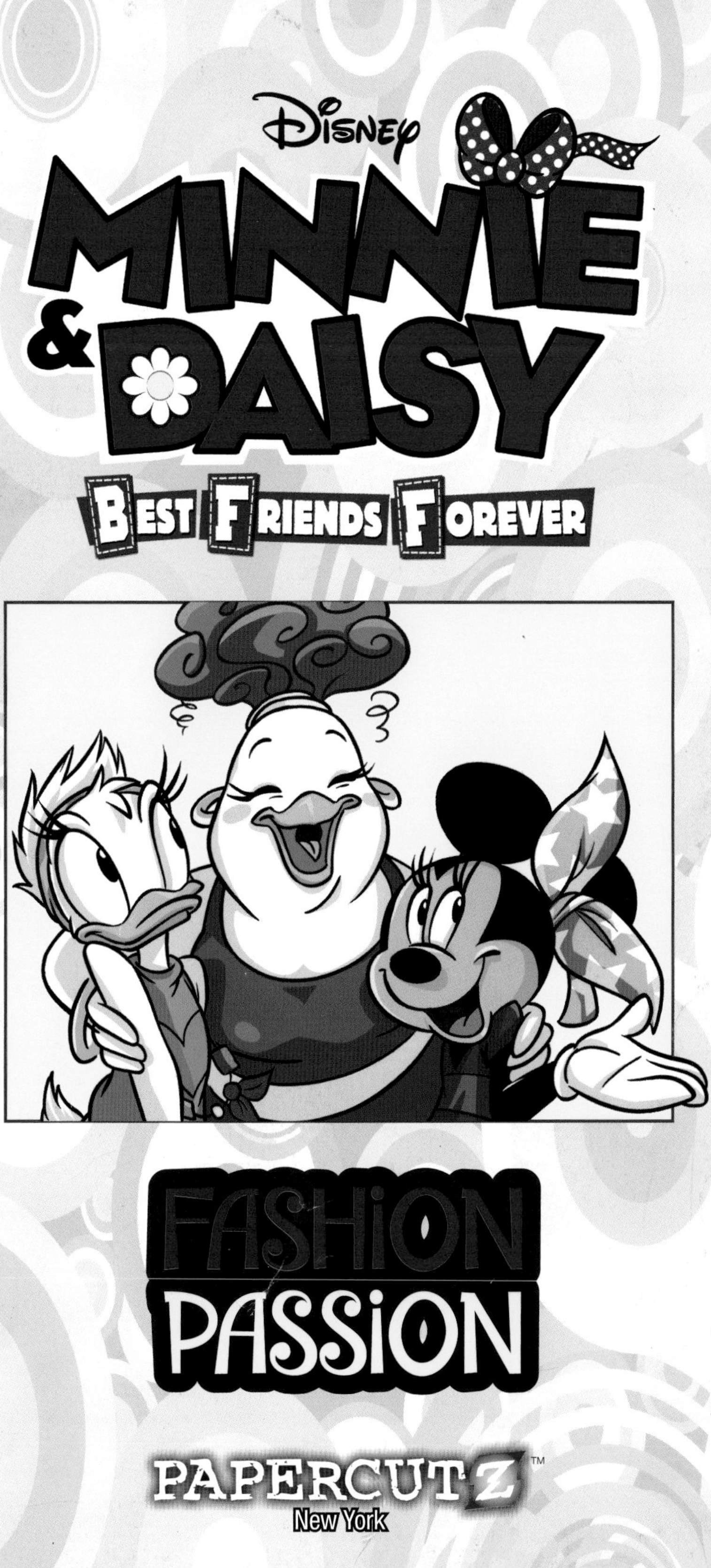

Fashion Passion

PAPERCUTZ™
New York

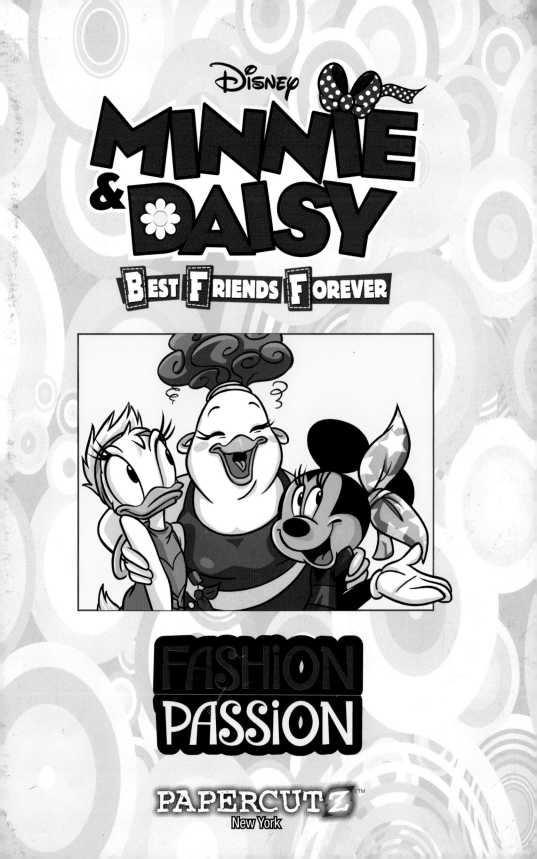

Contents

DISNEY GRAPHIC NOVELS #6
"Minnie & Daisy: Fashion Passion"
Dawn K. Guzzo - Design/Production
Robert V. Conte - Editor
Jeff Whitman - Assistant Managing Editor
Jim Salicrup
Editor-in-Chief

Special Thanks to Carlotta Quattrocolo,
Arianna Marchione, Krista Wong, and
Eugene Paraszczuk at Disney Enterprises, Inc.

ISBN: 978-1-62991-752-8 Paperback Edition
ISBN: 978-1-62991-753-5 Hardcover Edition
Copyright © 2017 by Disney Enterprises, Inc.
All rights reserved.

Printed in Korea
March 2017

Papercutz books may be purchased for business or promotional use.
For information on bulk purchases please contact
Macmillan Corporate and Premium Sales Department at (800) 221-7945 x5442.

Distributed by Macmillan
First Papercutz Printing

Disney Minnie & Daisy Best Friends Forever

Fashion Passion

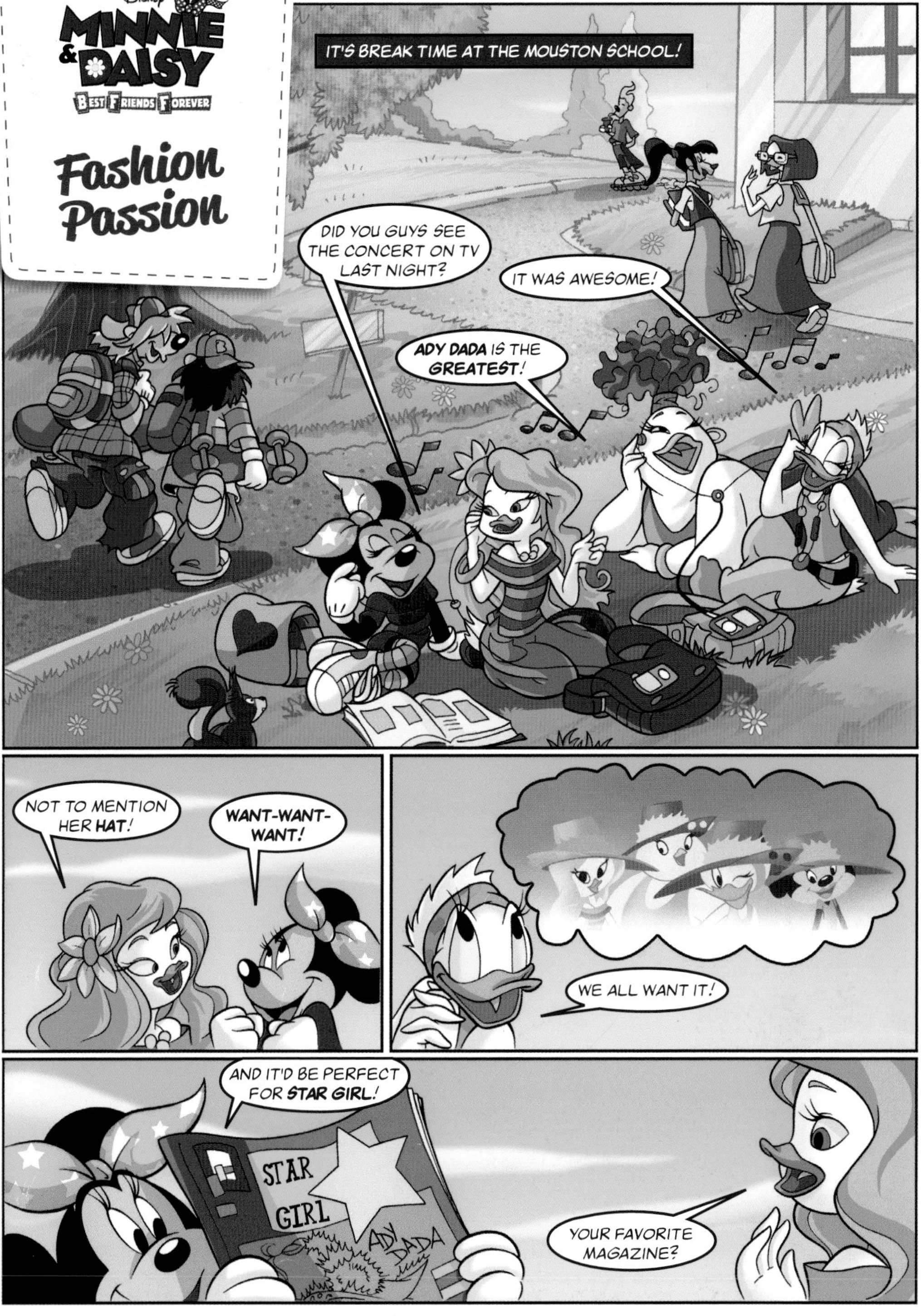
IT'S BREAK TIME AT THE MOUSTON SCHOOL!
DID YOU GUYS SEE THE CONCERT ON TV LAST NIGHT?
IT WAS AWESOME!
ADY DADA IS THE GREATEST!
NOT TO MENTION HER HAT!
WANT-WANT-WANT!
WE ALL WANT IT!
AND IT'D BE PERFECT FOR STAR GIRL!
STAR GIRL
ADY DADA
YOUR FAVORITE MAGAZINE?

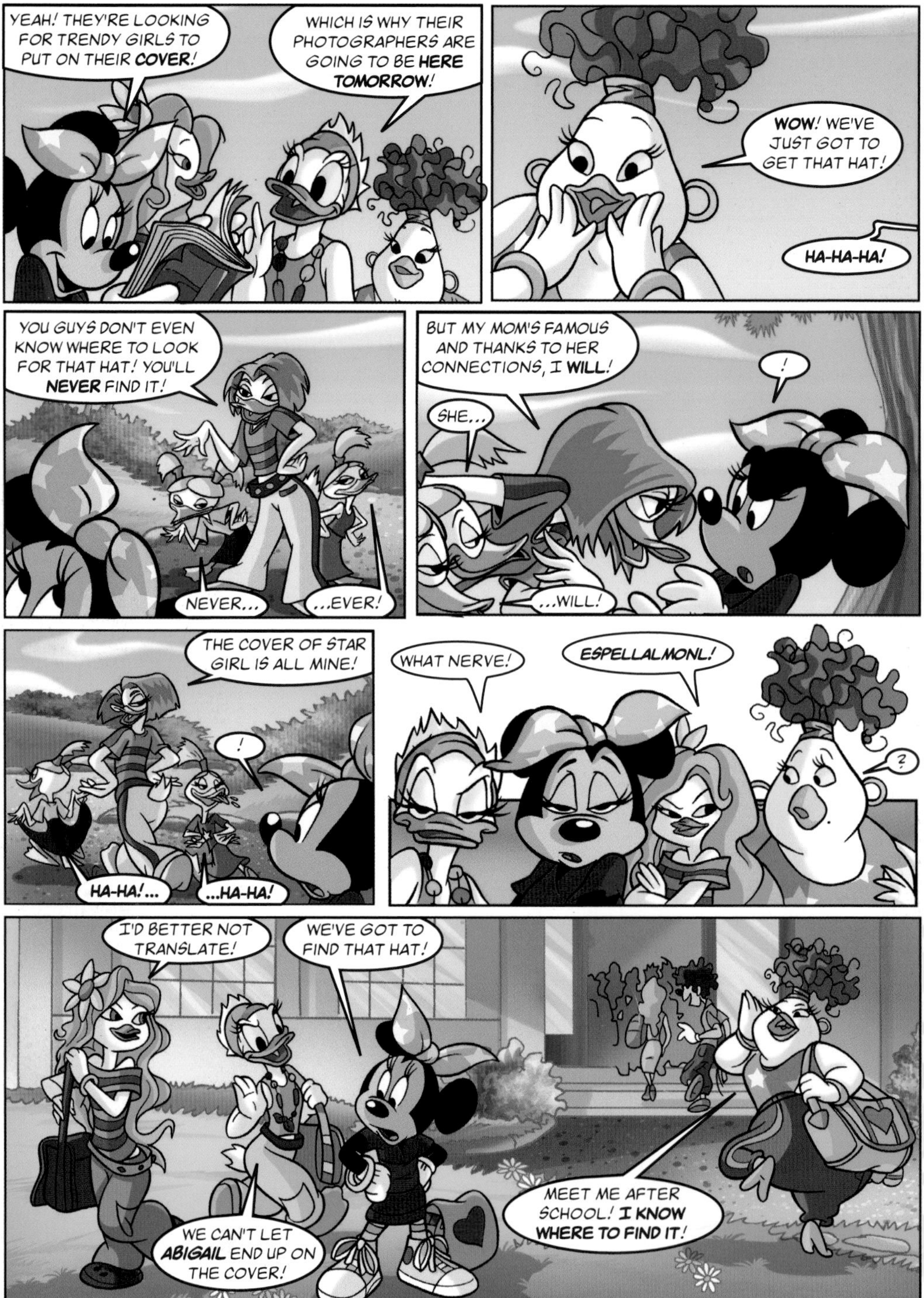
YEAH! THEY'RE LOOKING FOR TRENDY GIRLS TO PUT ON THEIR **COVER**!
WHICH IS WHY THEIR PHOTOGRAPHERS ARE GOING TO BE **HERE TOMORROW**!
WOW! WE'VE JUST GOT TO GET THAT HAT!
HA-HA-HA!
YOU GUYS DON'T EVEN KNOW WHERE TO LOOK FOR THAT HAT! YOU'LL **NEVER** FIND IT!
NEVER...
...EVER!
BUT MY MOM'S FAMOUS AND THANKS TO HER CONNECTIONS, I **WILL**!
!
SHE...
...WILL!
THE COVER OF STAR GIRL IS ALL MINE!
!
HA-HA!...
...HA-HA!
WHAT NERVE!
ESPELLALMONL!
?
I'D BETTER NOT TRANSLATE!
WE'VE GOT TO FIND THAT HAT!
WE CAN'T LET **ABIGAIL** END UP ON THE COVER!
MEET ME AFTER SCHOOL! **I KNOW WHERE TO FIND IT**!

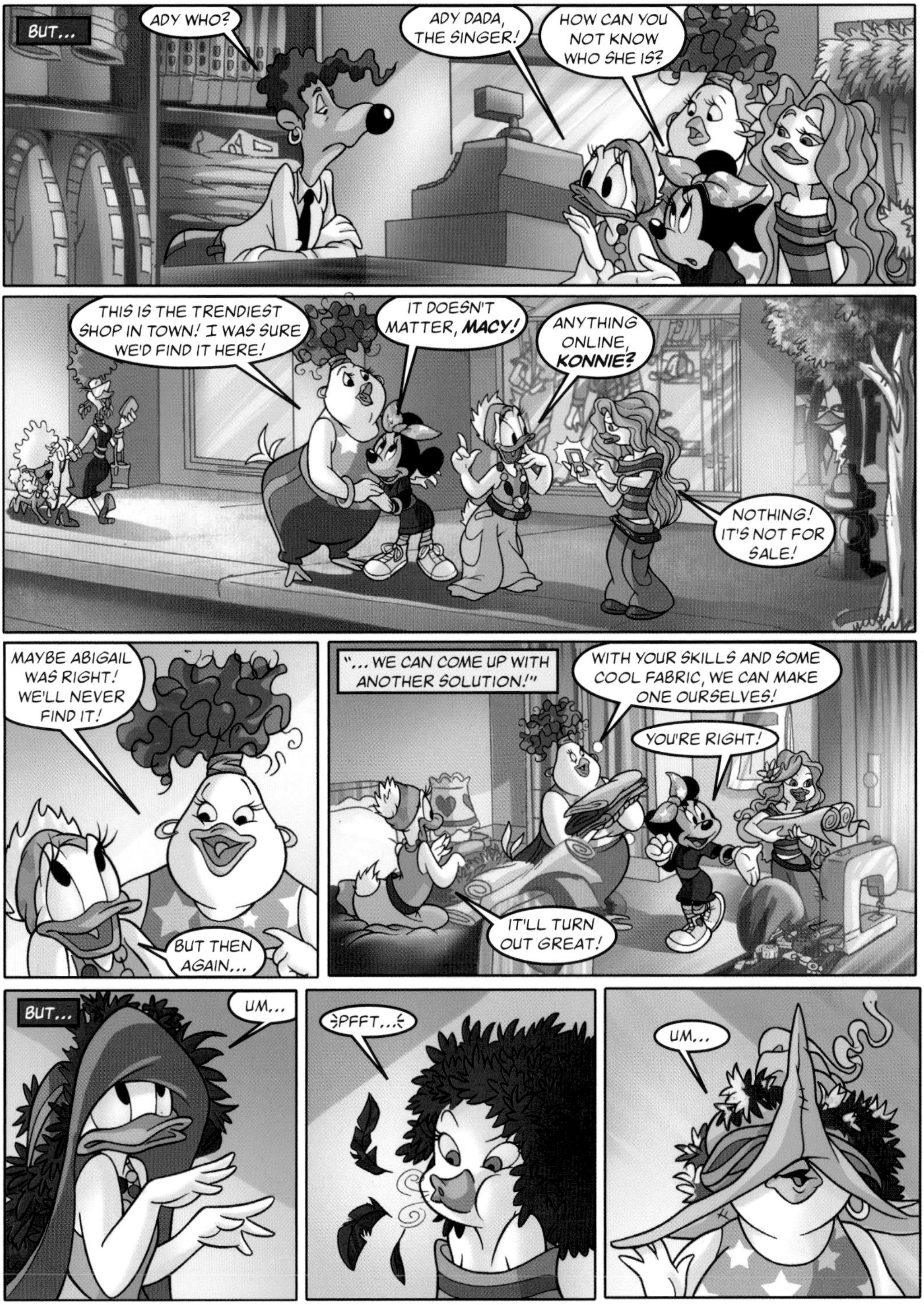
BUT...
ADY WHO?
ADY DADA, THE SINGER!
HOW CAN YOU NOT KNOW WHO SHE IS?
THIS IS THE TRENDIEST SHOP IN TOWN! I WAS SURE WE'D FIND IT HERE!
IT DOESN'T MATTER, **MACY!**
ANYTHING ONLINE, **KONNIE?**
NOTHING! IT'S NOT FOR SALE!
MAYBE ABIGAIL WAS RIGHT! WE'LL NEVER FIND IT!
BUT THEN AGAIN...
"...WE CAN COME UP WITH ANOTHER SOLUTION!"
WITH YOUR SKILLS AND SOME COOL FABRIC, WE CAN MAKE ONE OURSELVES!
YOU'RE RIGHT!
IT'LL TURN OUT GREAT!
BUT...
UM...
PFFT...
UM...

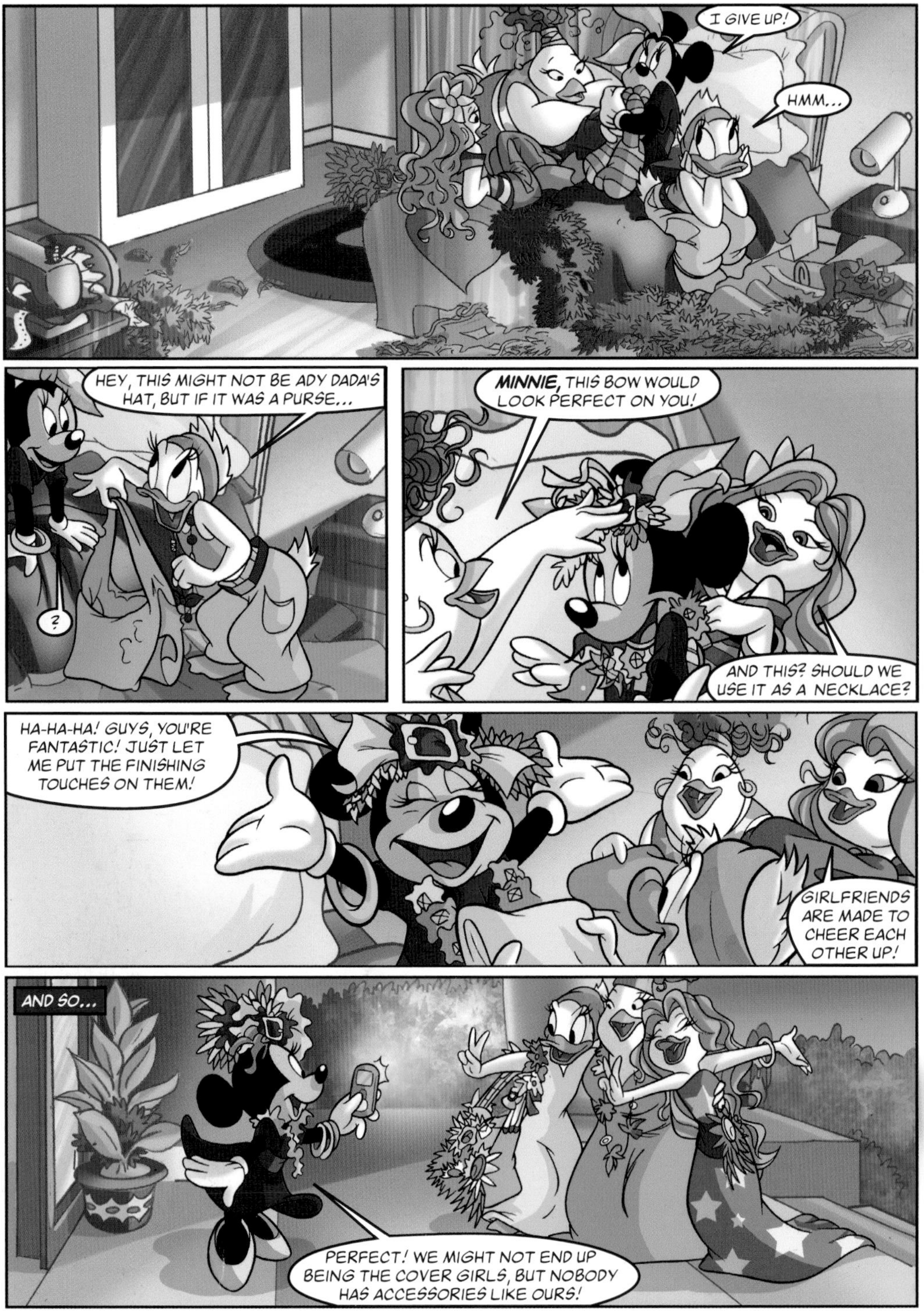
I GIVE UP!
HMM...
HEY, THIS MIGHT NOT BE ADY DADA'S HAT, BUT IF IT WAS A PURSE...
?
MINNIE, THIS BOW WOULD LOOK PERFECT ON YOU!
AND THIS? SHOULD WE USE IT AS A NECKLACE?
HA-HA-HA! GUYS, YOU'RE FANTASTIC! JUST LET ME PUT THE FINISHING TOUCHES ON THEM!
GIRLFRIENDS ARE MADE TO CHEER EACH OTHER UP!
AND SO...
PERFECT! WE MIGHT NOT END UP BEING THE COVER GIRLS, BUT NOBODY HAS ACCESSORIES LIKE OURS!

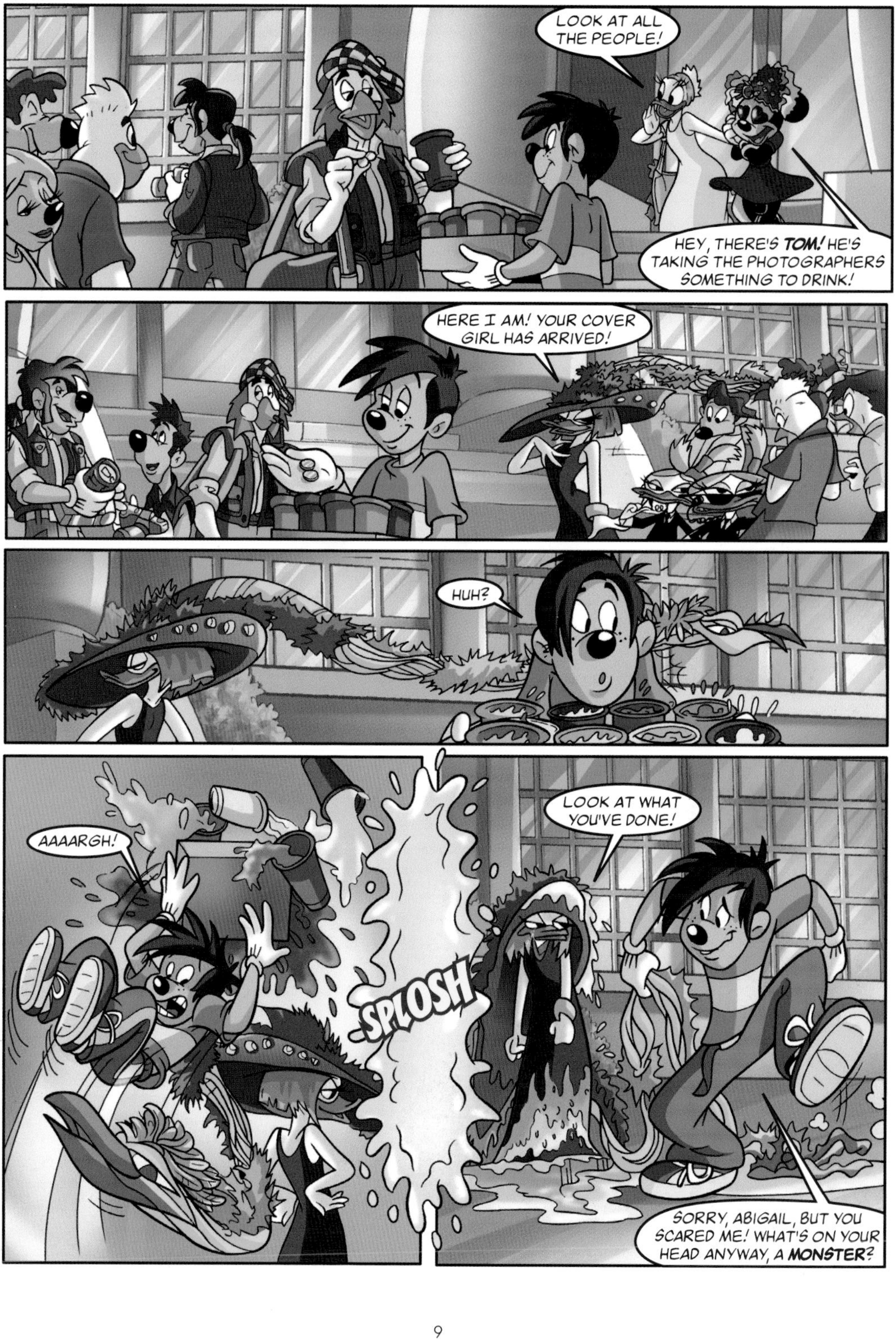
LOOK AT ALL THE PEOPLE!
HEY, THERE'S **TOM!** HE'S TAKING THE PHOTOGRAPHERS SOMETHING TO DRINK!
HERE I AM! YOUR COVER GIRL HAS ARRIVED!
HUH?
AAAARGH!
SPLOSH
LOOK AT WHAT YOU'VE DONE!
SORRY, ABIGAIL, BUT YOU SCARED ME! WHAT'S ON YOUR HEAD ANYWAY, A **MONSTER**?

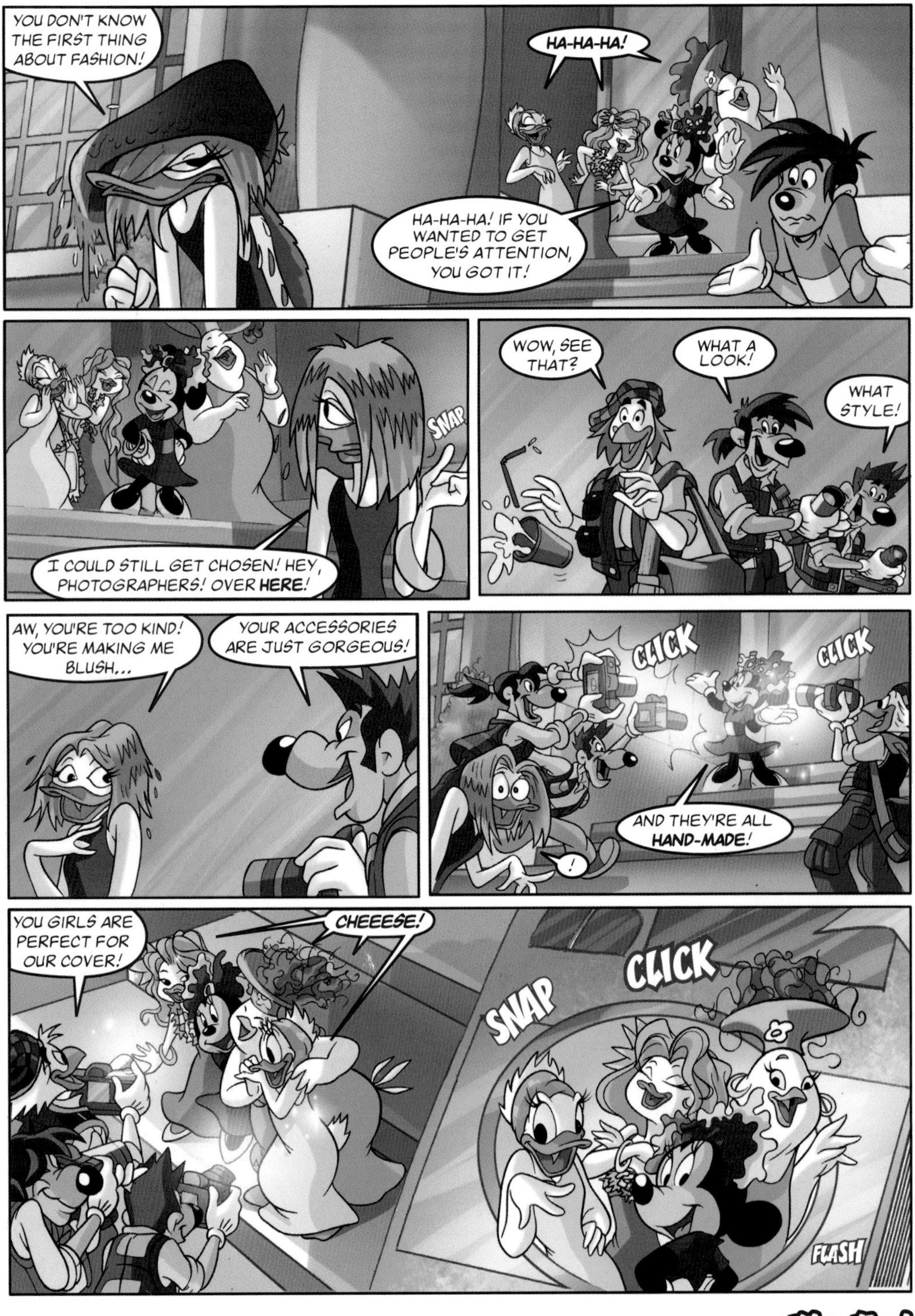
YOU DON'T KNOW THE FIRST THING ABOUT FASHION!
HA-HA-HA!
HA-HA-HA! IF YOU WANTED TO GET PEOPLE'S ATTENTION, YOU GOT IT!
SNAP
I COULD STILL GET CHOSEN! HEY, PHOTOGRAPHERS! OVER HERE!
WOW, SEE THAT?
WHAT A LOOK!
WHAT STYLE!
AW, YOU'RE TOO KIND! YOU'RE MAKING ME BLUSH...
YOUR ACCESSORIES ARE JUST GORGEOUS!
CLICK
CLICK
AND THEY'RE ALL HAND-MADE!
!
YOU GIRLS ARE PERFECT FOR OUR COVER!
CHEEESE!
SNAP
CLICK
FLASH

The End

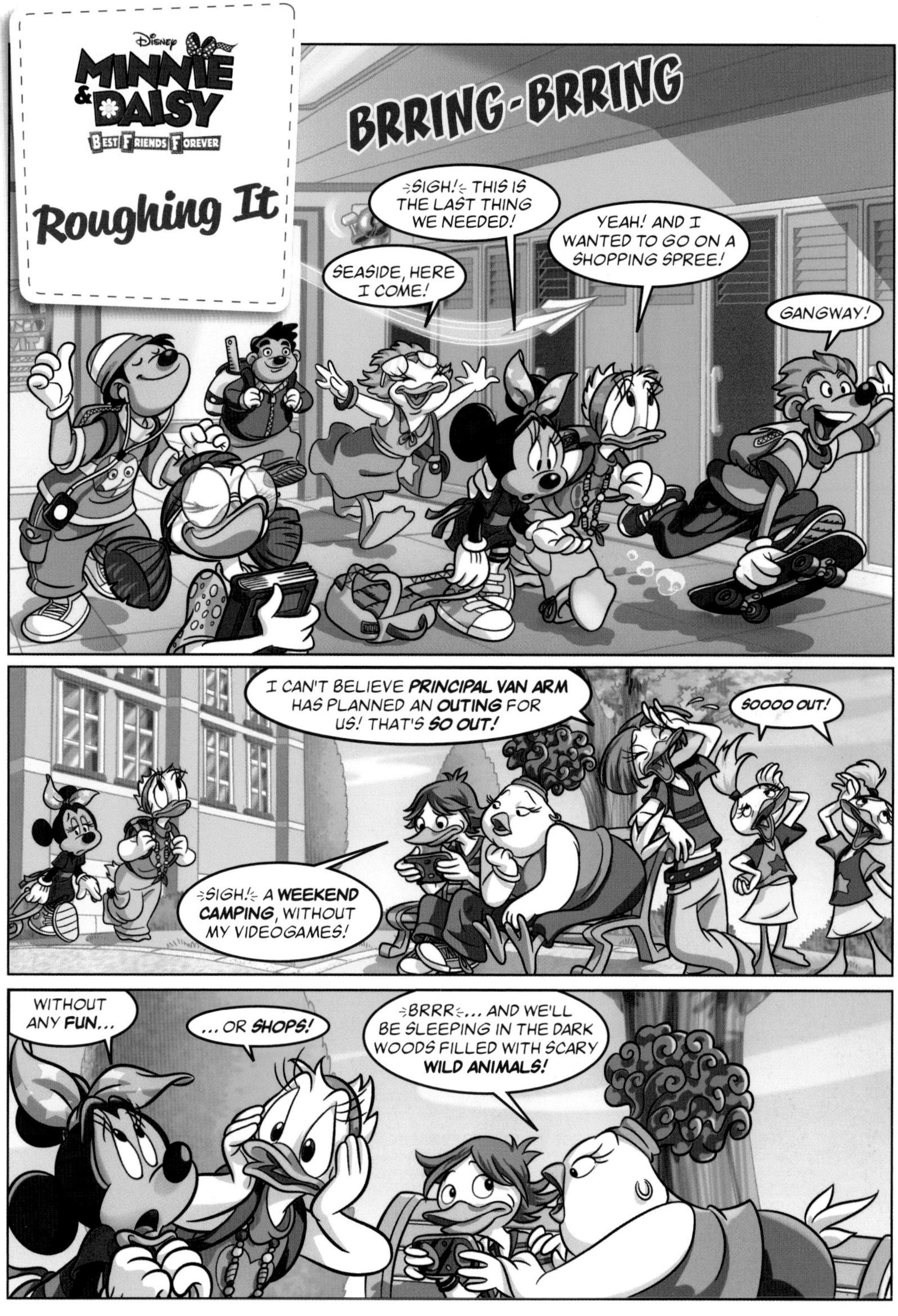

DISNEY MINNIE & DAISY BEST FRIENDS FOREVER
Roughing It
BRRING-BRRING
SEASIDE, HERE I COME!
SIGH! THIS IS THE LAST THING WE NEEDED!
YEAH! AND I WANTED TO GO ON A SHOPPING SPREE!
GANGWAY!
I CAN'T BELIEVE **PRINCIPAL VAN ARM** HAS PLANNED AN **OUTING** FOR US! THAT'S **SO OUT!**
SOOOO OUT!
SIGH! A **WEEKEND CAMPING**, WITHOUT MY VIDEOGAMES!
WITHOUT ANY **FUN...**
... OR **SHOPS!**
BRRR... AND WE'LL BE SLEEPING IN THE DARK WOODS FILLED WITH SCARY **WILD ANIMALS!**

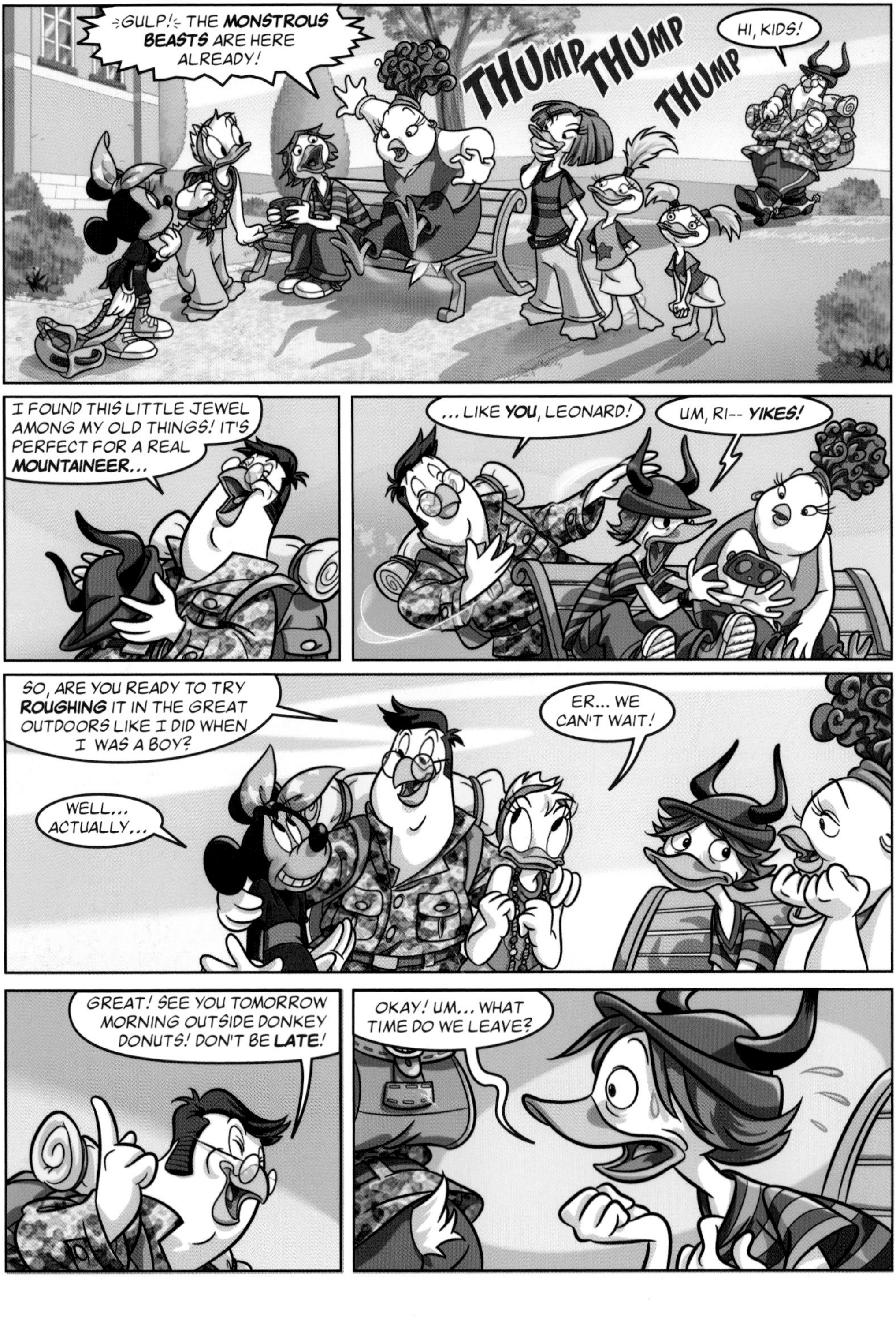

GULP! THE MONSTROUS BEASTS ARE HERE ALREADY!
THUMP THUMP THUMP
HI, KIDS!
I FOUND THIS LITTLE JEWEL AMONG MY OLD THINGS! IT'S PERFECT FOR A REAL MOUNTAINEER...
...LIKE YOU, LEONARD!
UM, RI-- YIKES!
SO, ARE YOU READY TO TRY ROUGHING IT IN THE GREAT OUTDOORS LIKE I DID WHEN I WAS A BOY?
WELL... ACTUALLY...
ER... WE CAN'T WAIT!
GREAT! SEE YOU TOMORROW MORNING OUTSIDE DONKEY DONUTS! DON'T BE LATE!
OKAY! UM... WHAT TIME DO WE LEAVE?

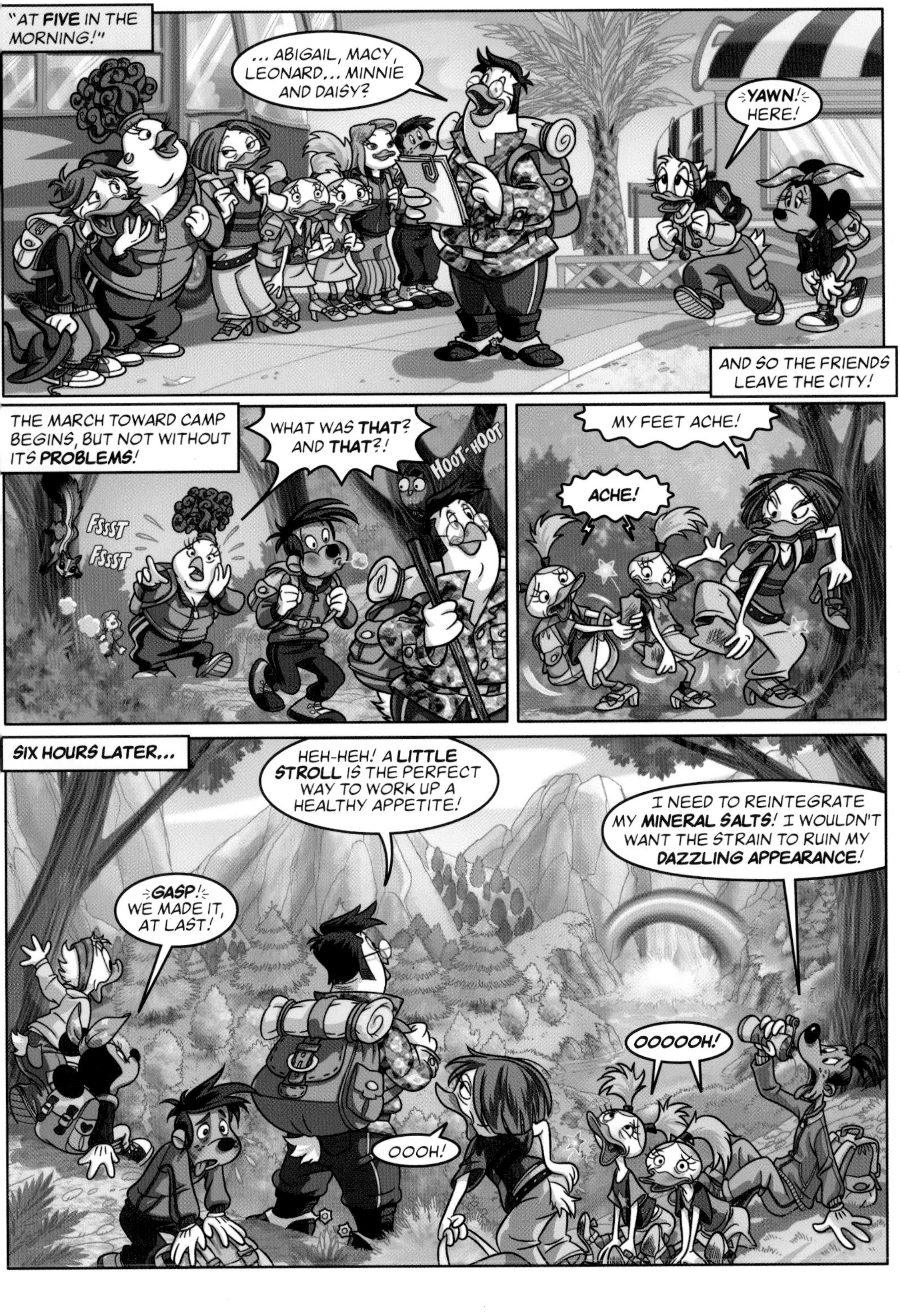
"AT FIVE IN THE MORNING!"
... ABIGAIL, MACY, LEONARD... MINNIE AND DAISY?
YAWN! HERE!
AND SO THE FRIENDS LEAVE THE CITY!
THE MARCH TOWARD CAMP BEGINS, BUT NOT WITHOUT ITS PROBLEMS!
FSSST FSSST
WHAT WAS THAT? AND THAT?!
HOOT-HOOT
MY FEET ACHE!
ACHE!
SIX HOURS LATER...
HEH-HEH! A LITTLE STROLL IS THE PERFECT WAY TO WORK UP A HEALTHY APPETITE!
I NEED TO REINTEGRATE MY MINERAL SALTS! I WOULDN'T WANT THE STRAIN TO RUIN MY DAZZLING APPEARANCE!
GASP! WE MADE IT, AT LAST!
OOOOOH!
OOOH!

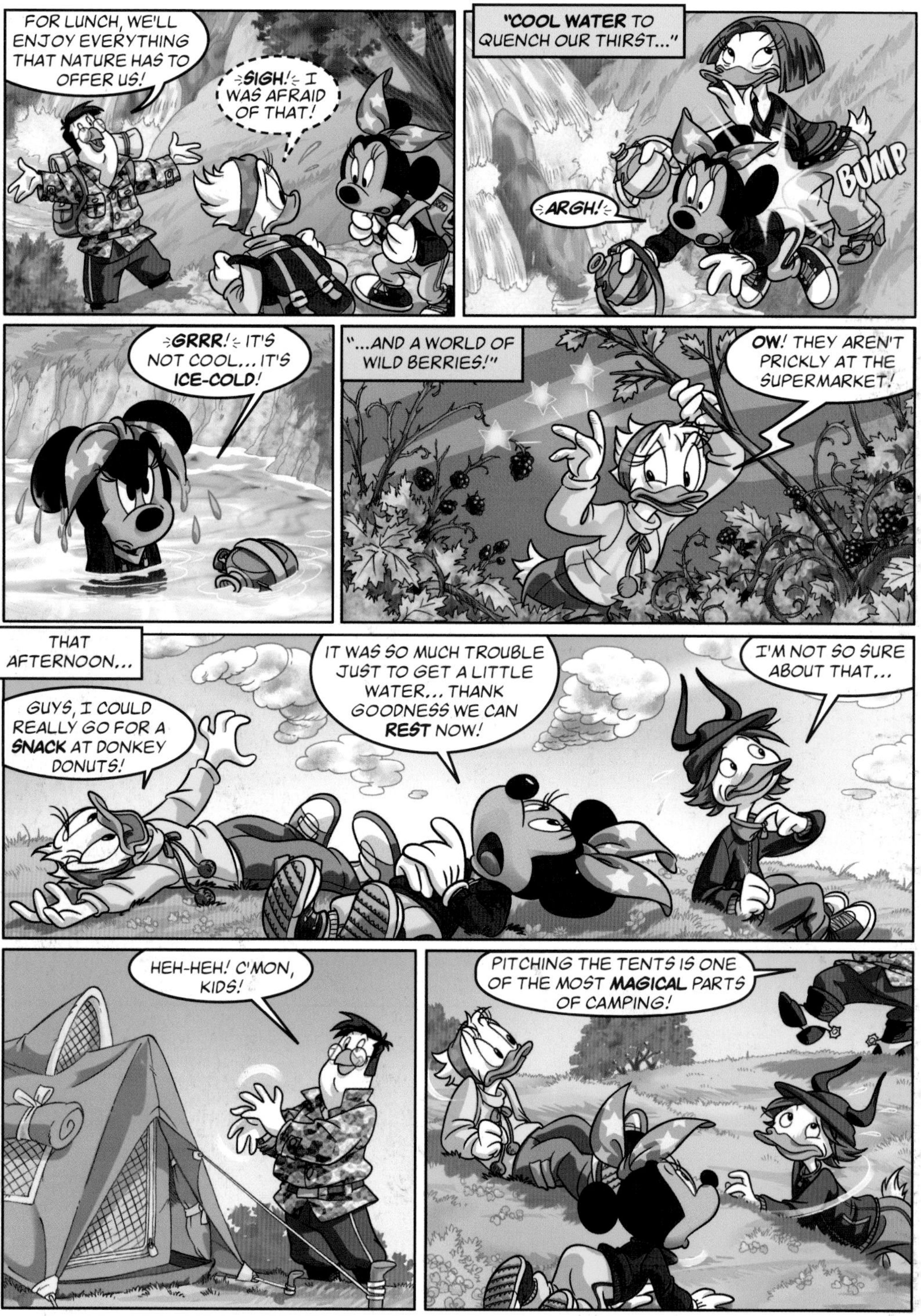
FOR LUNCH, WE'LL ENJOY EVERYTHING THAT NATURE HAS TO OFFER US!
SIGH! I WAS AFRAID OF THAT!
"COOL WATER TO QUENCH OUR THIRST..."
ARGH!
BUMP
GRRR! IT'S NOT COOL... IT'S ICE-COLD!
"...AND A WORLD OF WILD BERRIES!"
OW! THEY AREN'T PRICKLY AT THE SUPERMARKET!
THAT AFTERNOON...
GUYS, I COULD REALLY GO FOR A SNACK AT DONKEY DONUTS!
IT WAS SO MUCH TROUBLE JUST TO GET A LITTLE WATER... THANK GOODNESS WE CAN REST NOW!
I'M NOT SO SURE ABOUT THAT...
HEH-HEH! C'MON, KIDS!
PITCHING THE TENTS IS ONE OF THE MOST MAGICAL PARTS OF CAMPING!

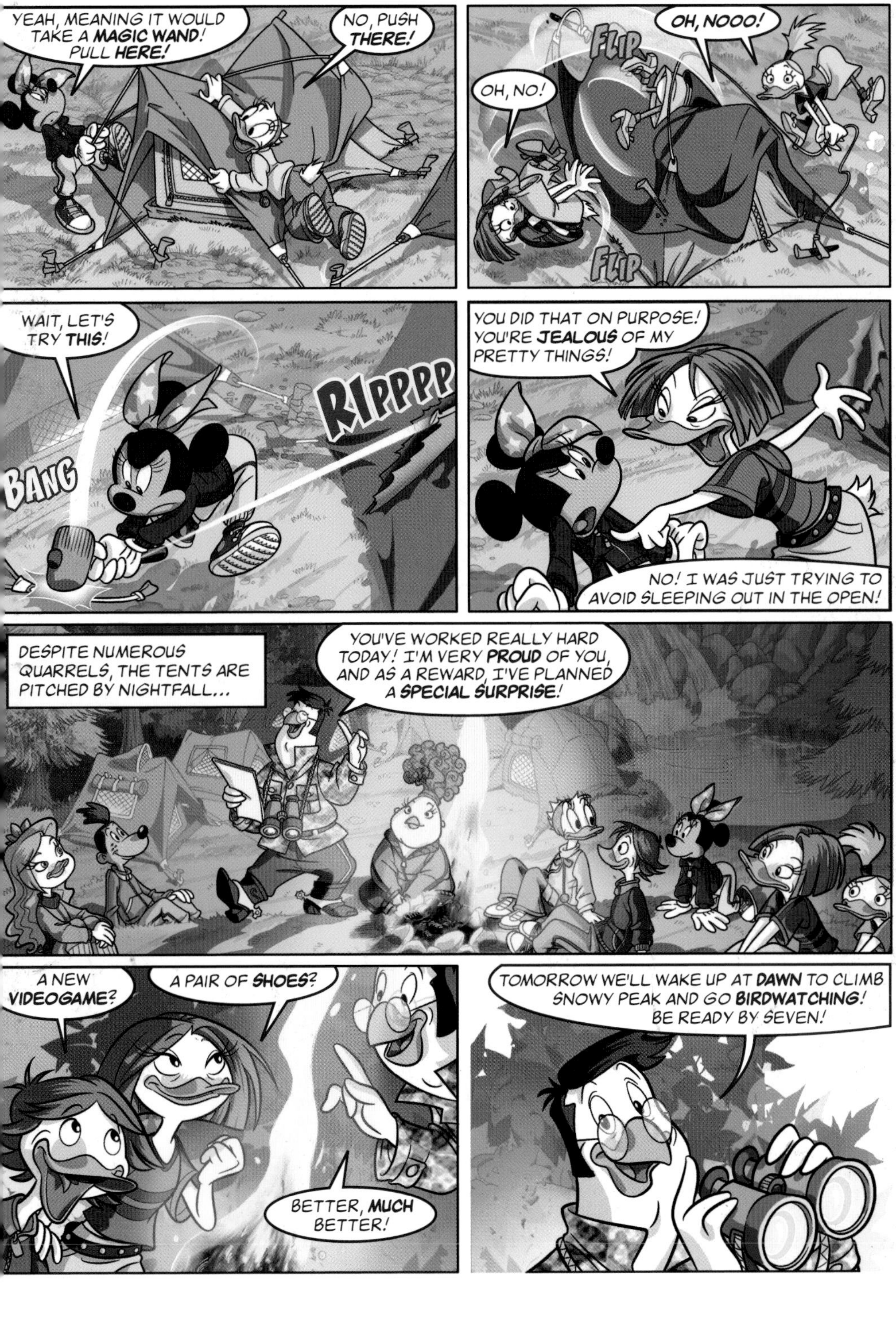
YEAH, MEANING IT WOULD TAKE A MAGIC WAND! PULL HERE!
NO, PUSH THERE!
FLIP
OH, NOOO!
OH, NO!
FLIP
WAIT, LET'S TRY THIS!
RIPPPP
BANG
YOU DID THAT ON PURPOSE! YOU'RE JEALOUS OF MY PRETTY THINGS!
NO! I WAS JUST TRYING TO AVOID SLEEPING OUT IN THE OPEN!
DESPITE NUMEROUS QUARRELS, THE TENTS ARE PITCHED BY NIGHTFALL...
YOU'VE WORKED REALLY HARD TODAY! I'M VERY PROUD OF YOU, AND AS A REWARD, I'VE PLANNED A SPECIAL SURPRISE!
A NEW VIDEOGAME?
A PAIR OF SHOES?
BETTER, MUCH BETTER!
TOMORROW WE'LL WAKE UP AT DAWN TO CLIMB SNOWY PEAK AND GO BIRDWATCHING! BE READY BY SEVEN!

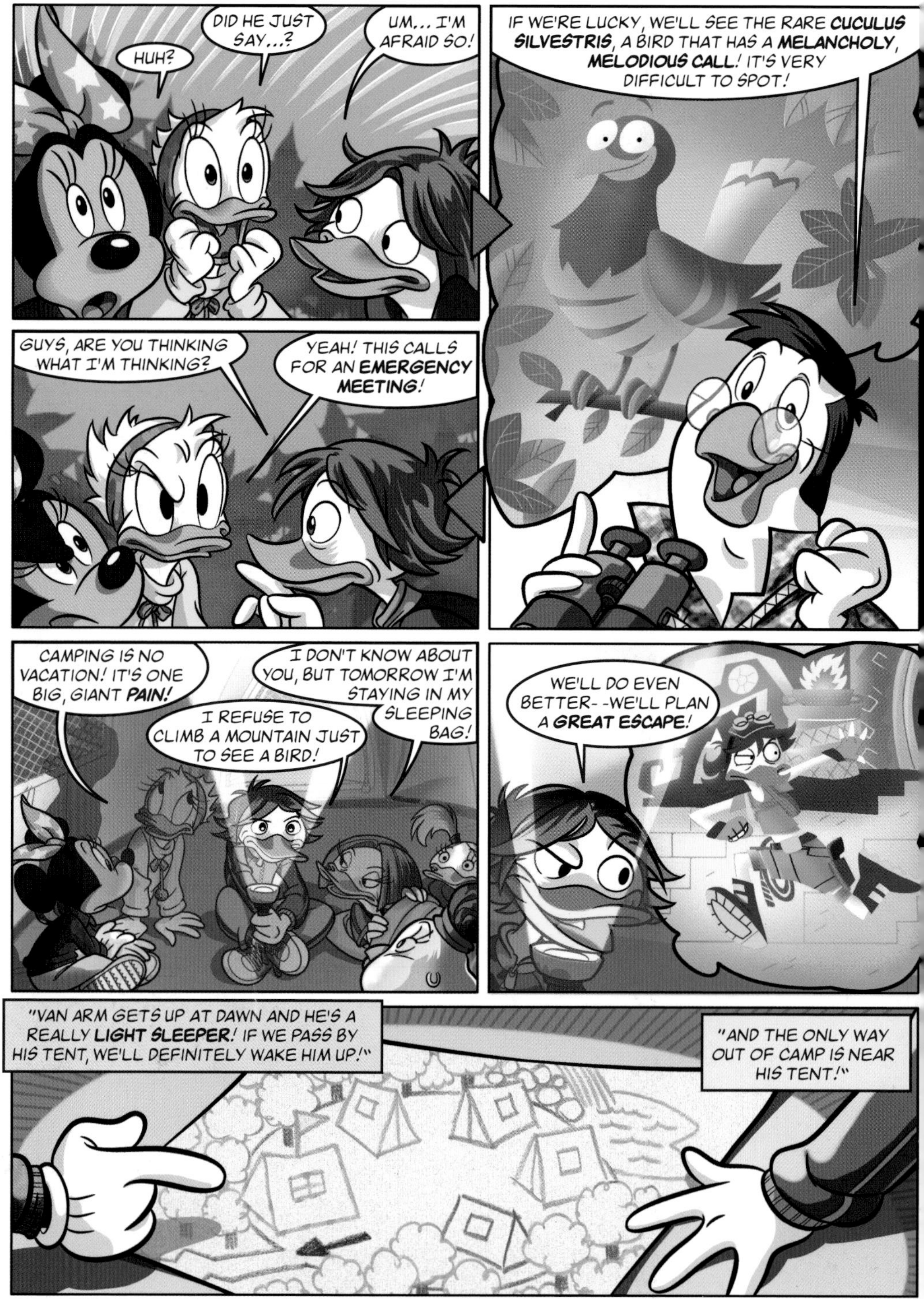
HUH?
DID HE JUST SAY...?
UM... I'M AFRAID SO!
IF WE'RE LUCKY, WE'LL SEE THE RARE **CUCULUS SILVESTRIS**, A BIRD THAT HAS A **MELANCHOLY, MELODIOUS CALL**! IT'S VERY DIFFICULT TO SPOT!
GUYS, ARE YOU THINKING WHAT I'M THINKING?
YEAH! THIS CALLS FOR AN **EMERGENCY MEETING**!
CAMPING IS NO VACATION! IT'S ONE BIG, GIANT **PAIN!**
I DON'T KNOW ABOUT YOU, BUT TOMORROW I'M STAYING IN MY SLEEPING BAG!
I REFUSE TO CLIMB A MOUNTAIN JUST TO SEE A BIRD!
WE'LL DO EVEN BETTER- -WE'LL PLAN A **GREAT ESCAPE**!
"VAN ARM GETS UP AT DAWN AND HE'S A REALLY **LIGHT SLEEPER**! IF WE PASS BY HIS TENT, WE'LL DEFINITELY WAKE HIM UP!"
"AND THE ONLY WAY OUT OF CAMP IS NEAR HIS TENT!"

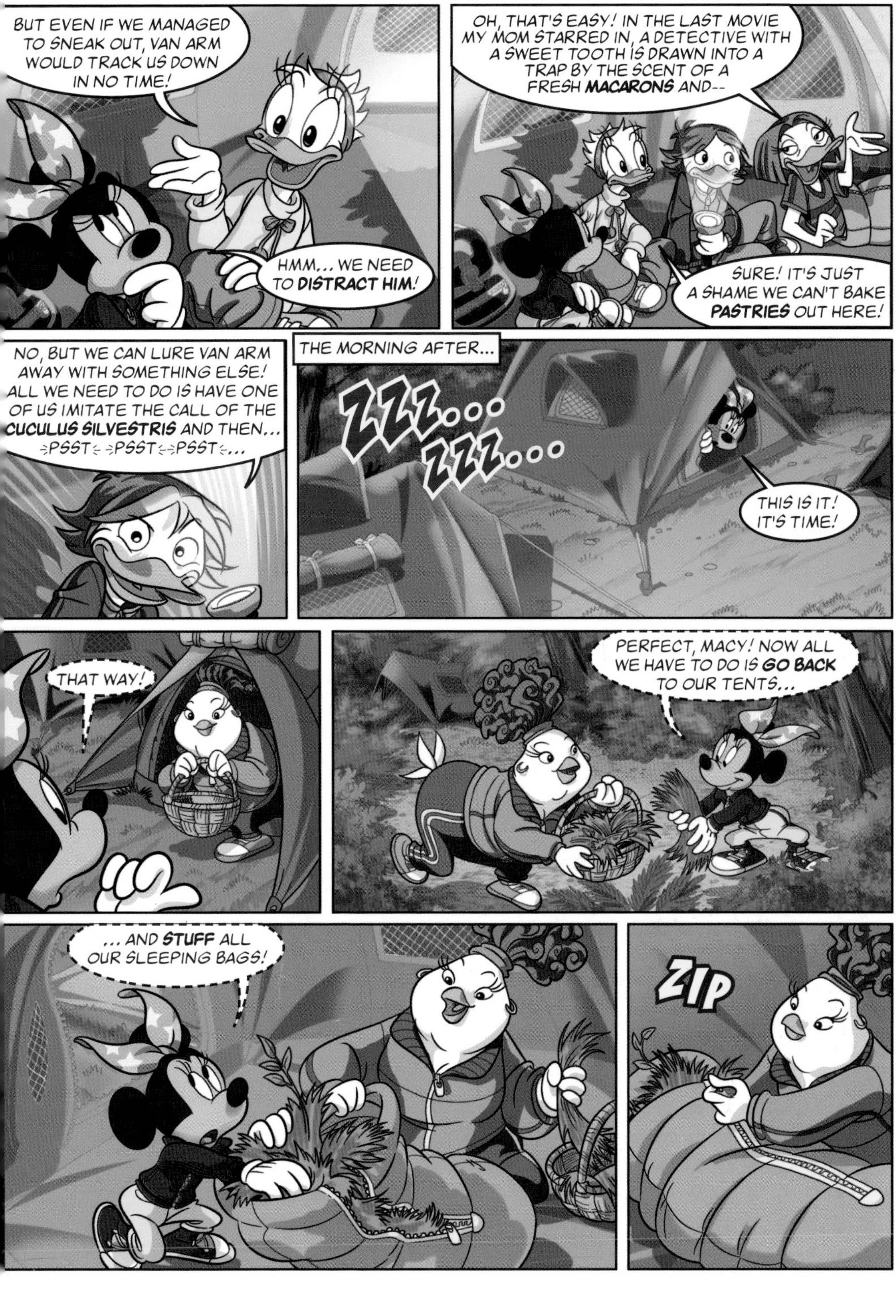
BUT EVEN IF WE MANAGED TO SNEAK OUT, VAN ARM WOULD TRACK US DOWN IN NO TIME!
HMM... WE NEED TO DISTRACT HIM!
OH, THAT'S EASY! IN THE LAST MOVIE MY MOM STARRED IN, A DETECTIVE WITH A SWEET TOOTH IS DRAWN INTO A TRAP BY THE SCENT OF A FRESH MACARONS AND--
SURE! IT'S JUST A SHAME WE CAN'T BAKE PASTRIES OUT HERE!
NO, BUT WE CAN LURE VAN ARM AWAY WITH SOMETHING ELSE! ALL WE NEED TO DO IS HAVE ONE OF US IMITATE THE CALL OF THE CUCULUS SILVESTRIS AND THEN... PSST PSST PSST...
THE MORNING AFTER...
ZZZ...
ZZZ...
THIS IS IT! IT'S TIME!
THAT WAY!
PERFECT, MACY! NOW ALL WE HAVE TO DO IS GO BACK TO OUR TENTS...
... AND STUFF ALL OUR SLEEPING BAGS!
ZIP

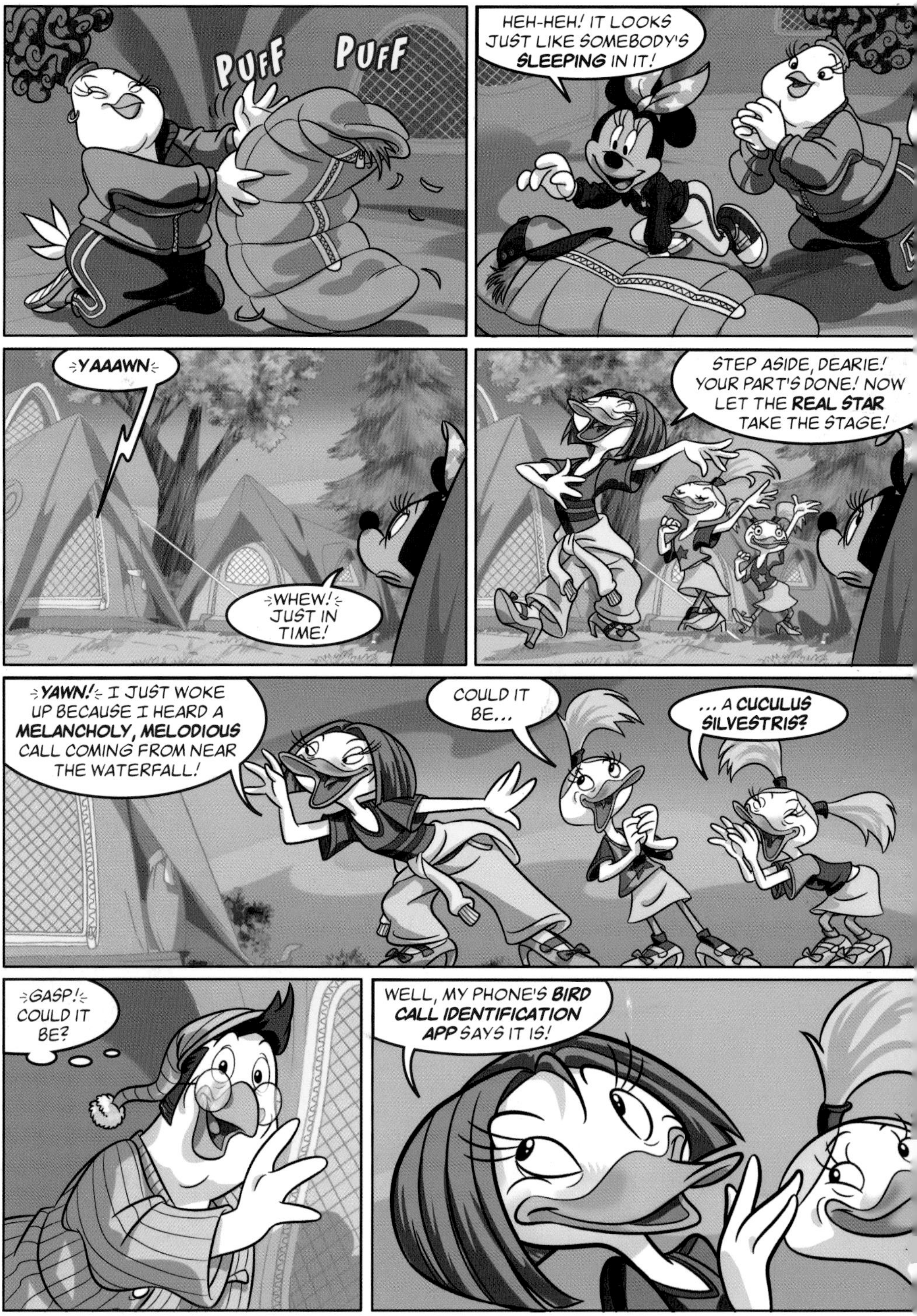
PUFF PUFF
HEH-HEH! IT LOOKS JUST LIKE SOMEBODY'S SLEEPING IN IT!
YAAAWN
WHEW! JUST IN TIME!
STEP ASIDE, DEARIE! YOUR PART'S DONE! NOW LET THE REAL STAR TAKE THE STAGE!
YAWN! I JUST WOKE UP BECAUSE I HEARD A MELANCHOLY, MELODIOUS CALL COMING FROM NEAR THE WATERFALL!
COULD IT BE...
... A CUCULUS SILVESTRIS?
GASP! COULD IT BE?
WELL, MY PHONE'S BIRD CALL IDENTIFICATION APP SAYS IT IS!

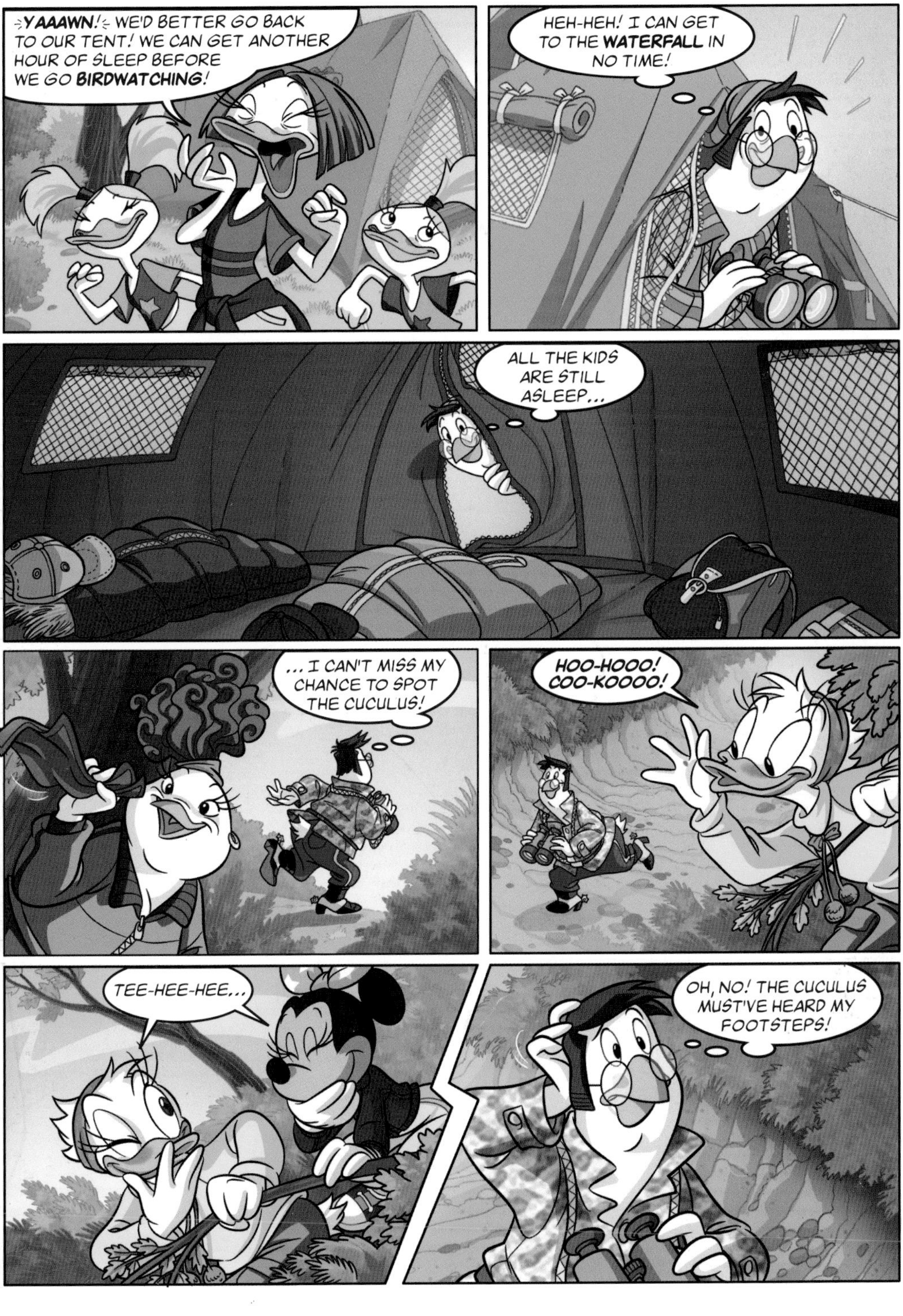

YAAAWN! WE'D BETTER GO BACK TO OUR TENT! WE CAN GET ANOTHER HOUR OF SLEEP BEFORE WE GO BIRDWATCHING!
HEH-HEH! I CAN GET TO THE WATERFALL IN NO TIME!
ALL THE KIDS ARE STILL ASLEEP...
...I CAN'T MISS MY CHANCE TO SPOT THE CUCULUS!
HOO-HOOO! COO-KOOOO!
TEE-HEE-HEE...
OH, NO! THE CUCULUS MUST'VE HEARD MY FOOTSTEPS!

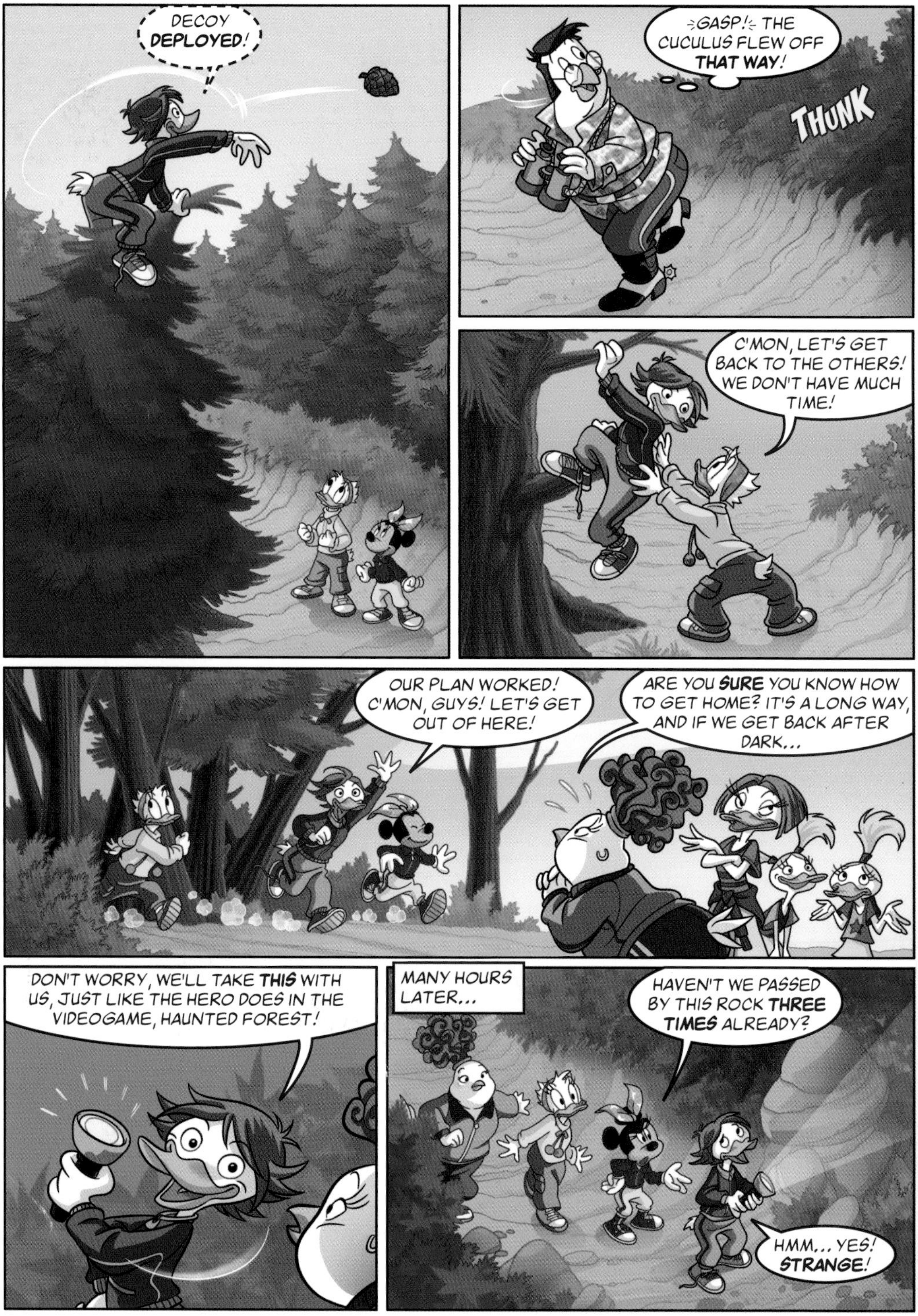
DECOY DEPLOYED!
GASP! THE CUCULUS FLEW OFF THAT WAY!
THUNK
C'MON, LET'S GET BACK TO THE OTHERS! WE DON'T HAVE MUCH TIME!
OUR PLAN WORKED! C'MON, GUYS! LET'S GET OUT OF HERE!
ARE YOU SURE YOU KNOW HOW TO GET HOME? IT'S A LONG WAY, AND IF WE GET BACK AFTER DARK...
DON'T WORRY, WE'LL TAKE THIS WITH US, JUST LIKE THE HERO DOES IN THE VIDEOGAME, HAUNTED FOREST!
MANY HOURS LATER...
HAVEN'T WE PASSED BY THIS ROCK THREE TIMES ALREADY?
HMM... YES! STRANGE!

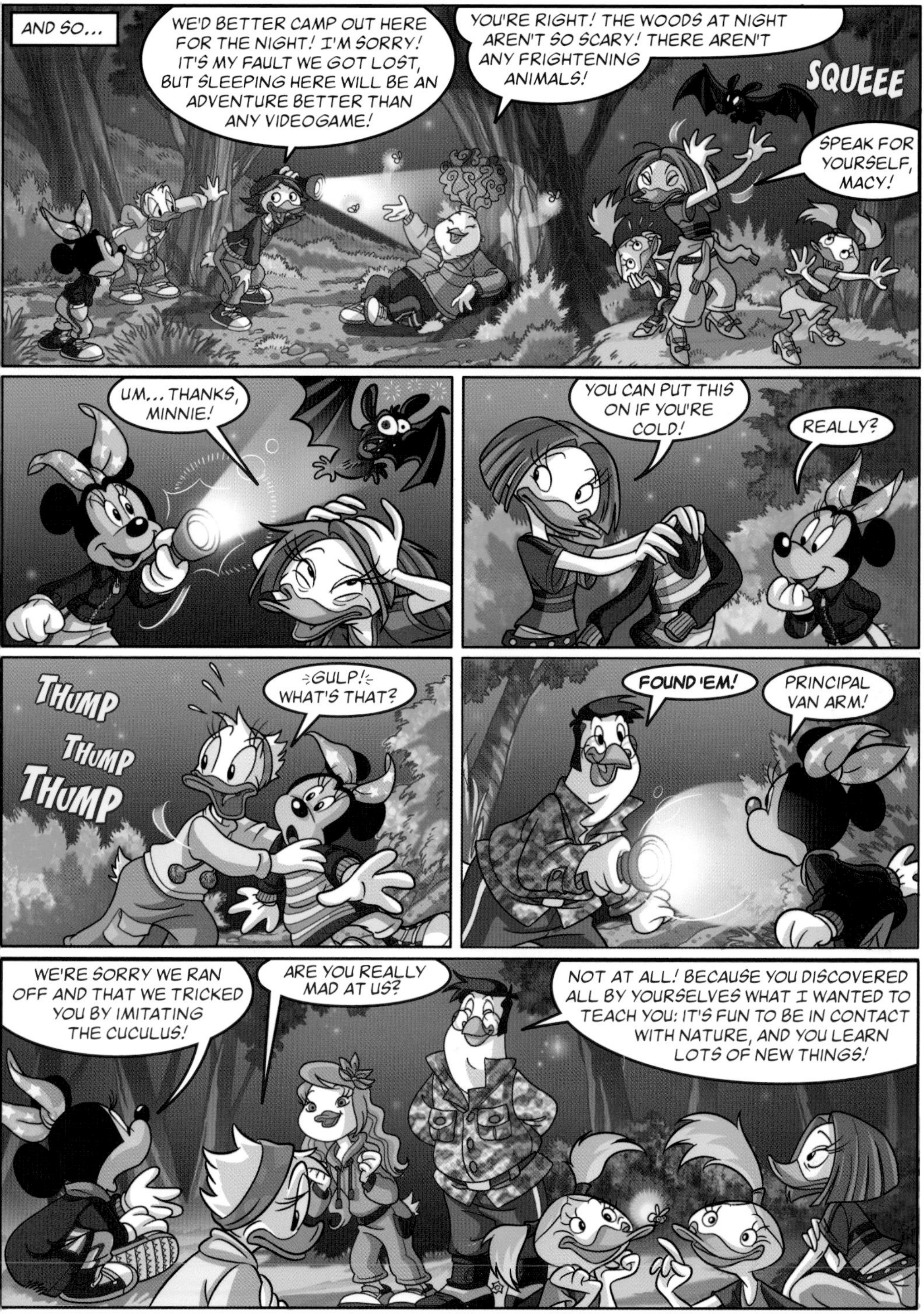
AND SO...
WE'D BETTER CAMP OUT HERE FOR THE NIGHT! I'M SORRY! IT'S MY FAULT WE GOT LOST, BUT SLEEPING HERE WILL BE AN ADVENTURE BETTER THAN ANY VIDEOGAME!
YOU'RE RIGHT! THE WOODS AT NIGHT AREN'T SO SCARY! THERE AREN'T ANY FRIGHTENING ANIMALS!
SQUEEE
SPEAK FOR YOURSELF, MACY!
UM... THANKS, MINNIE!
YOU CAN PUT THIS ON IF YOU'RE COLD!
REALLY?
THUMP
THUMP
THUMP
GULP! WHAT'S THAT?
FOUND 'EM!
PRINCIPAL VAN ARM!
WE'RE SORRY WE RAN OFF AND THAT WE TRICKED YOU BY IMITATING THE CUCULUS!
ARE YOU REALLY MAD AT US?
NOT AT ALL! BECAUSE YOU DISCOVERED ALL BY YOURSELVES WHAT I WANTED TO TEACH YOU: IT'S FUN TO BE IN CONTACT WITH NATURE, AND YOU LEARN LOTS OF NEW THINGS!

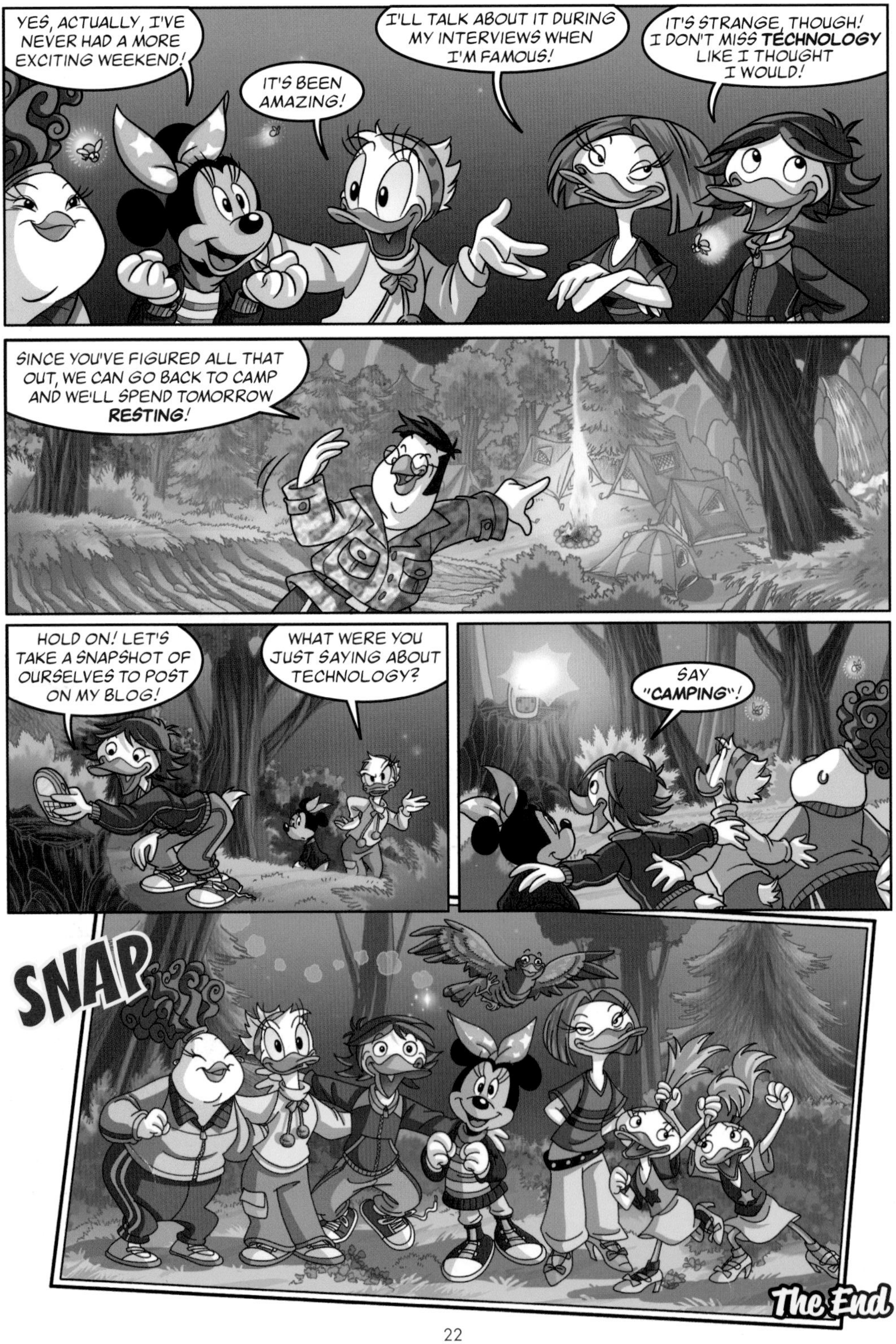
YES, ACTUALLY, I'VE NEVER HAD A MORE EXCITING WEEKEND!
IT'S BEEN AMAZING!
I'LL TALK ABOUT IT DURING MY INTERVIEWS WHEN I'M FAMOUS!
IT'S STRANGE, THOUGH! I DON'T MISS **TECHNOLOGY** LIKE I THOUGHT I WOULD!
SINCE YOU'VE FIGURED ALL THAT OUT, WE CAN GO BACK TO CAMP AND WE'LL SPEND TOMORROW **RESTING**!
HOLD ON! LET'S TAKE A SNAPSHOT OF OURSELVES TO POST ON MY BLOG!
WHAT WERE YOU JUST SAYING ABOUT TECHNOLOGY?
SAY "**CAMPING**"!
SNAP
The End

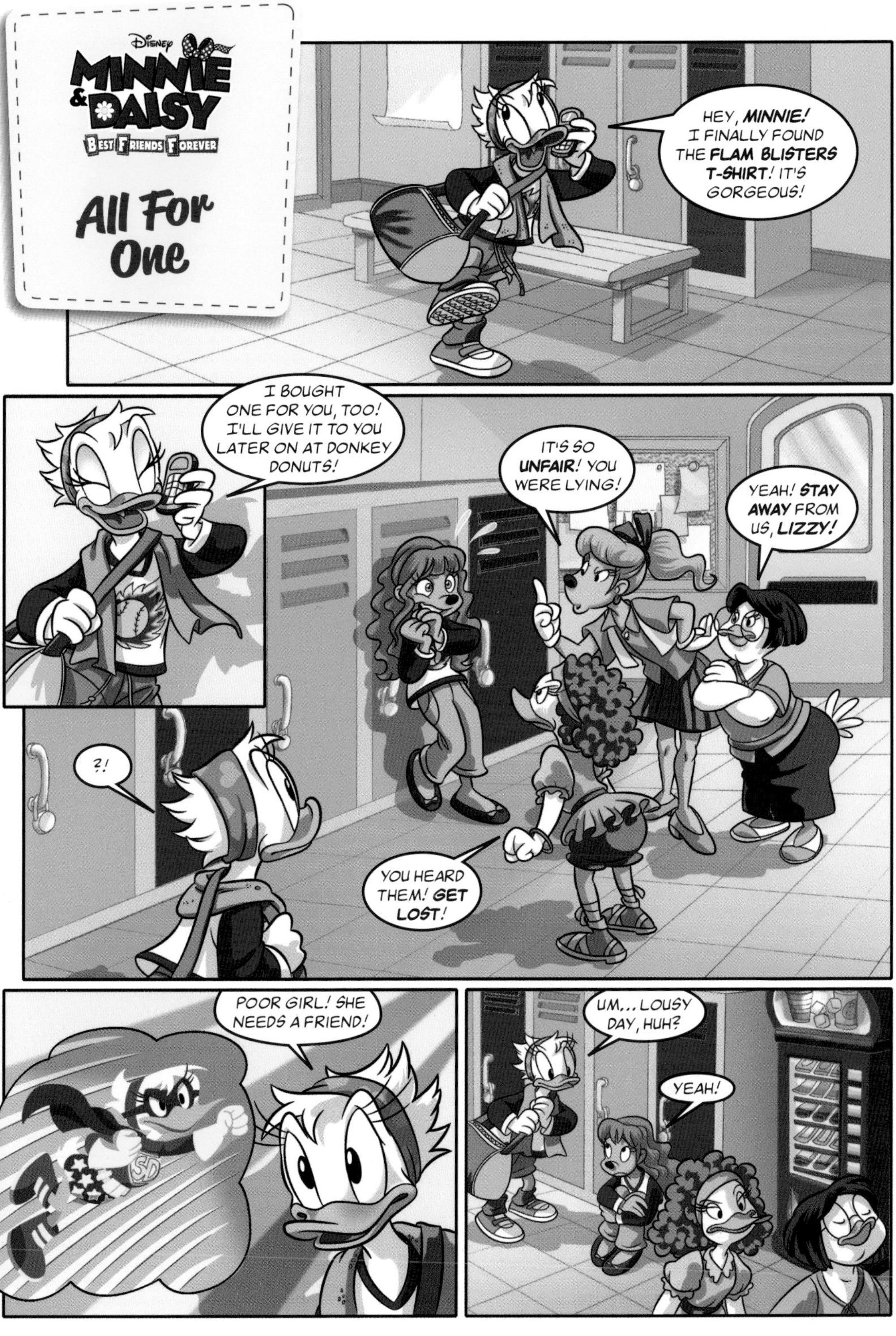
DISNEY MINNIE & DAISY BEST FRIENDS FOREVER
All For One
HEY, MINNIE! I FINALLY FOUND THE FLAM BLISTERS T-SHIRT! IT'S GORGEOUS!
I BOUGHT ONE FOR YOU, TOO! I'LL GIVE IT TO YOU LATER ON AT DONKEY DONUTS!
IT'S SO UNFAIR! YOU WERE LYING!
YEAH! STAY AWAY FROM US, LIZZY!
?!
YOU HEARD THEM! GET LOST!
POOR GIRL! SHE NEEDS A FRIEND!
UM... LOUSY DAY, HUH?
YEAH!

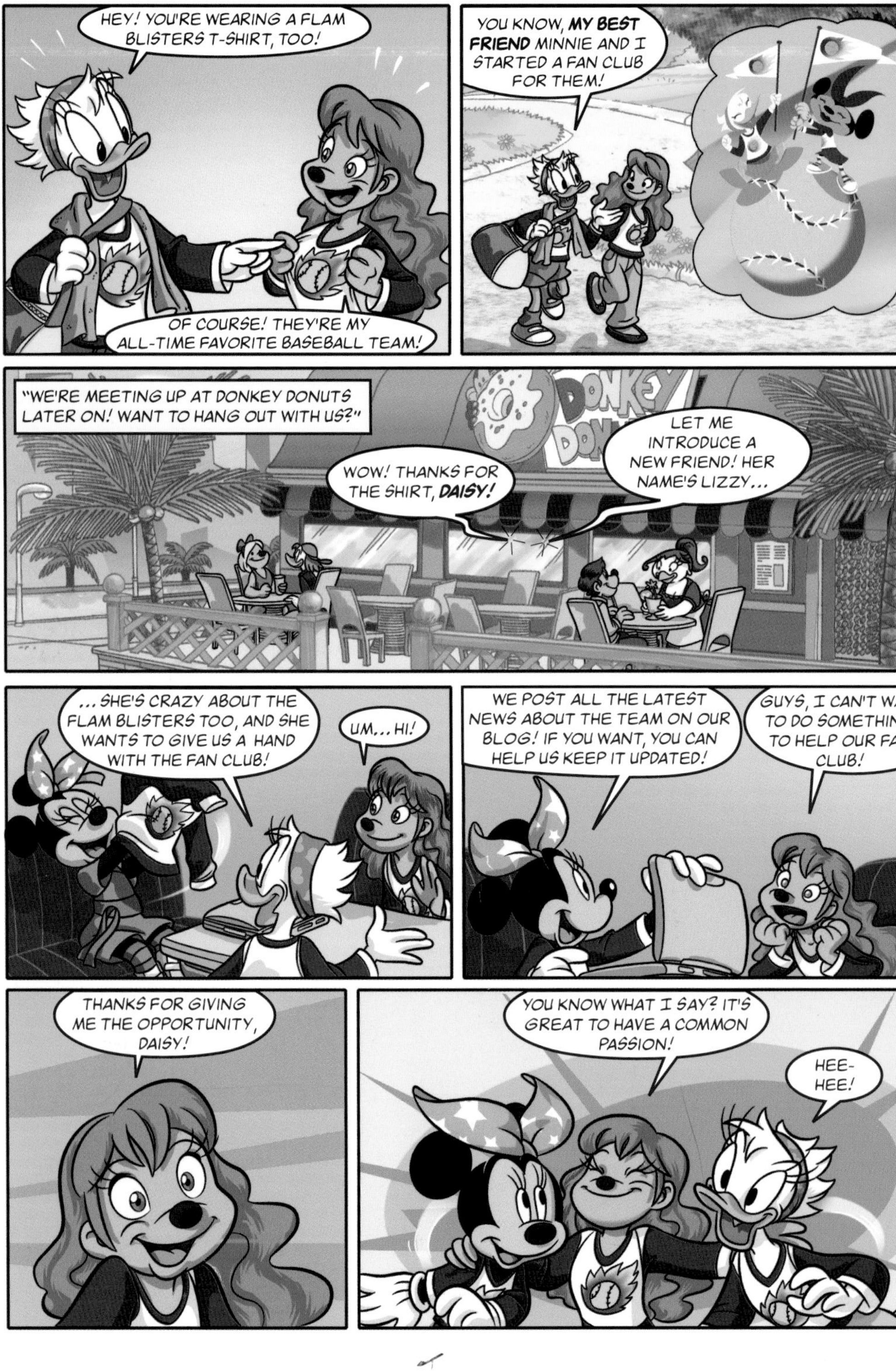
HEY! YOU'RE WEARING A FLAM BLISTERS T-SHIRT, TOO!
OF COURSE! THEY'RE MY ALL-TIME FAVORITE BASEBALL TEAM!
YOU KNOW, MY BEST FRIEND MINNIE AND I STARTED A FAN CLUB FOR THEM!
"WE'RE MEETING UP AT DONKEY DONUTS LATER ON! WANT TO HANG OUT WITH US?"
WOW! THANKS FOR THE SHIRT, DAISY!
LET ME INTRODUCE A NEW FRIEND! HER NAME'S LIZZY...
...SHE'S CRAZY ABOUT THE FLAM BLISTERS TOO, AND SHE WANTS TO GIVE US A HAND WITH THE FAN CLUB!
UM... HI!
WE POST ALL THE LATEST NEWS ABOUT THE TEAM ON OUR BLOG! IF YOU WANT, YOU CAN HELP US KEEP IT UPDATED!
GUYS, I CAN'T WAIT TO DO SOMETHING TO HELP OUR FAN CLUB!
THANKS FOR GIVING ME THE OPPORTUNITY, DAISY!
YOU KNOW WHAT I SAY? IT'S GREAT TO HAVE A COMMON PASSION!
HEE-HEE!

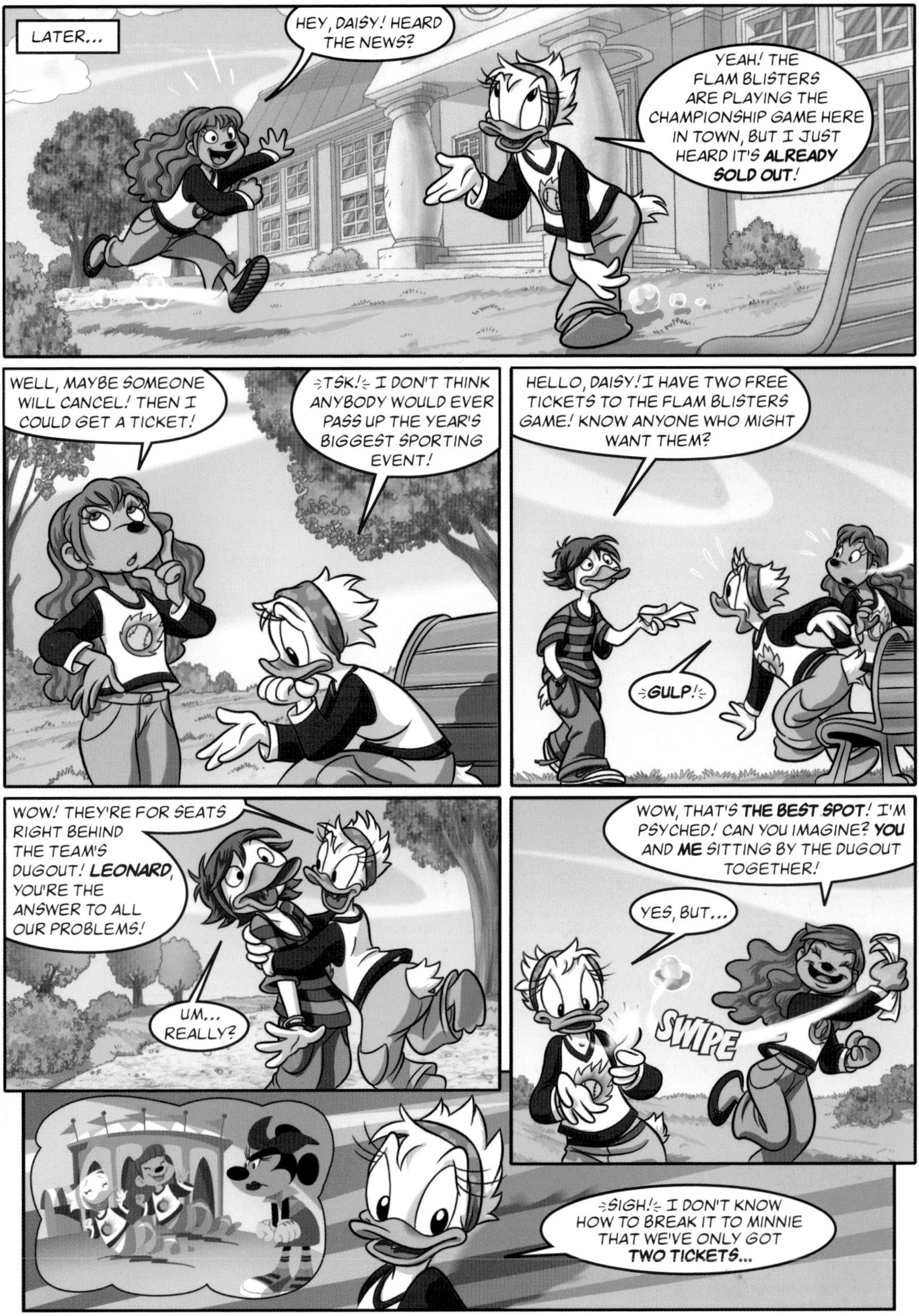
LATER...
HEY, DAISY! HEARD THE NEWS?
YEAH! THE FLAM BLISTERS ARE PLAYING THE CHAMPIONSHIP GAME HERE IN TOWN, BUT I JUST HEARD IT'S **ALREADY SOLD OUT**!
WELL, MAYBE SOMEONE WILL CANCEL! THEN I COULD GET A TICKET!
TSK! I DON'T THINK ANYBODY WOULD EVER PASS UP THE YEAR'S BIGGEST SPORTING EVENT!
HELLO, DAISY! I HAVE TWO FREE TICKETS TO THE FLAM BLISTERS GAME! KNOW ANYONE WHO MIGHT WANT THEM?
GULP!
WOW! THEY'RE FOR SEATS RIGHT BEHIND THE TEAM'S DUGOUT! **LEONARD**, YOU'RE THE ANSWER TO ALL OUR PROBLEMS!
UM... REALLY?
WOW, THAT'S **THE BEST SPOT**! I'M PSYCHED! CAN YOU IMAGINE? **YOU** AND **ME** SITTING BY THE DUGOUT TOGETHER!
YES, BUT...
SWIPE
SIGH! I DON'T KNOW HOW TO BREAK IT TO MINNIE THAT WE'VE ONLY GOT **TWO TICKETS...**

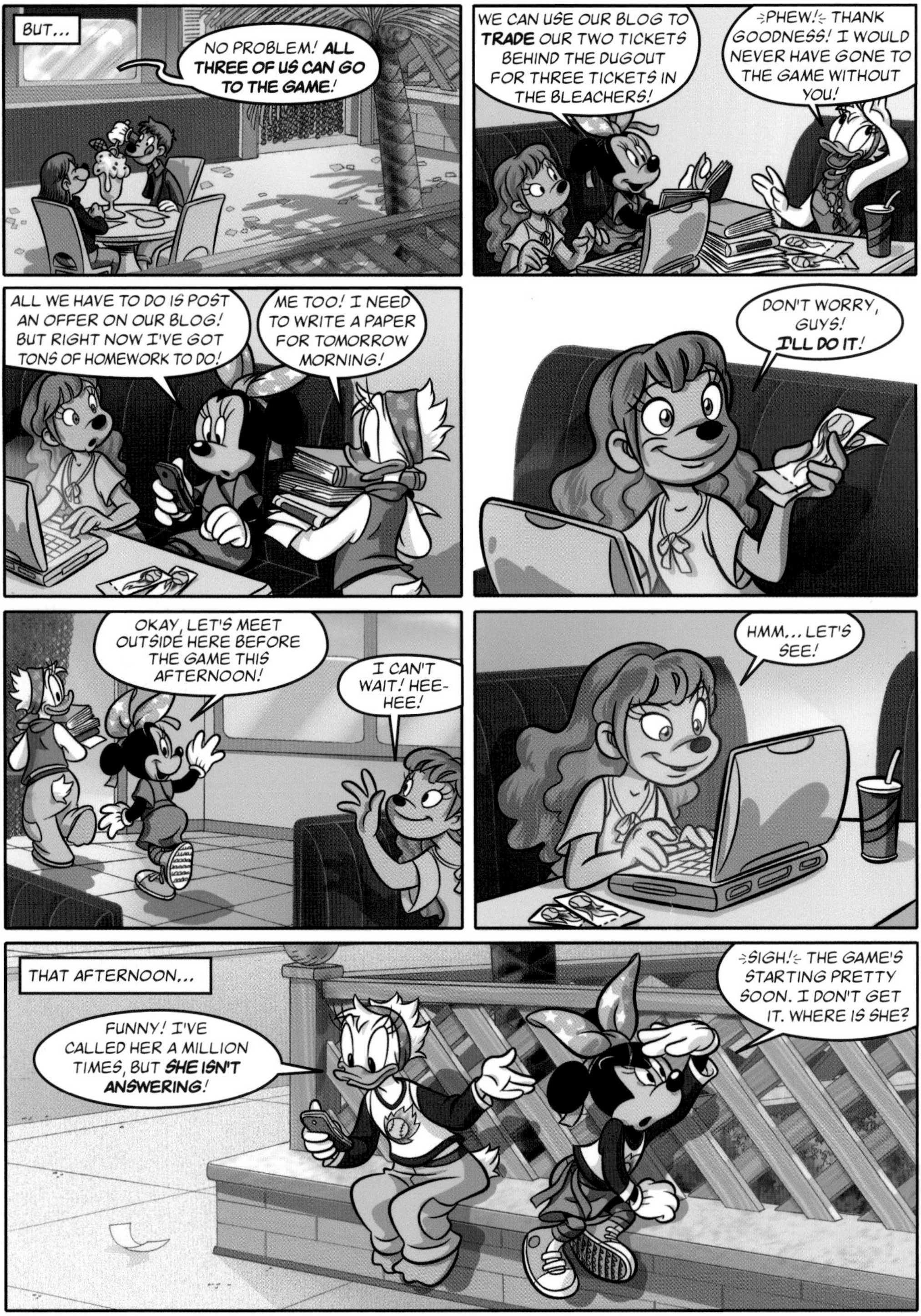
BUT...
NO PROBLEM! ALL THREE OF US CAN GO TO THE GAME!
WE CAN USE OUR BLOG TO TRADE OUR TWO TICKETS BEHIND THE DUGOUT FOR THREE TICKETS IN THE BLEACHERS!
PHEW! THANK GOODNESS! I WOULD NEVER HAVE GONE TO THE GAME WITHOUT YOU!
ALL WE HAVE TO DO IS POST AN OFFER ON OUR BLOG! BUT RIGHT NOW I'VE GOT TONS OF HOMEWORK TO DO!
ME TOO! I NEED TO WRITE A PAPER FOR TOMORROW MORNING!
DON'T WORRY, GUYS! I'LL DO IT!
OKAY, LET'S MEET OUTSIDE HERE BEFORE THE GAME THIS AFTERNOON!
I CAN'T WAIT! HEE-HEE!
HMM... LET'S SEE!
THAT AFTERNOON...
FUNNY! I'VE CALLED HER A MILLION TIMES, BUT SHE ISN'T ANSWERING!
SIGH! THE GAME'S STARTING PRETTY SOON. I DON'T GET IT. WHERE IS SHE?

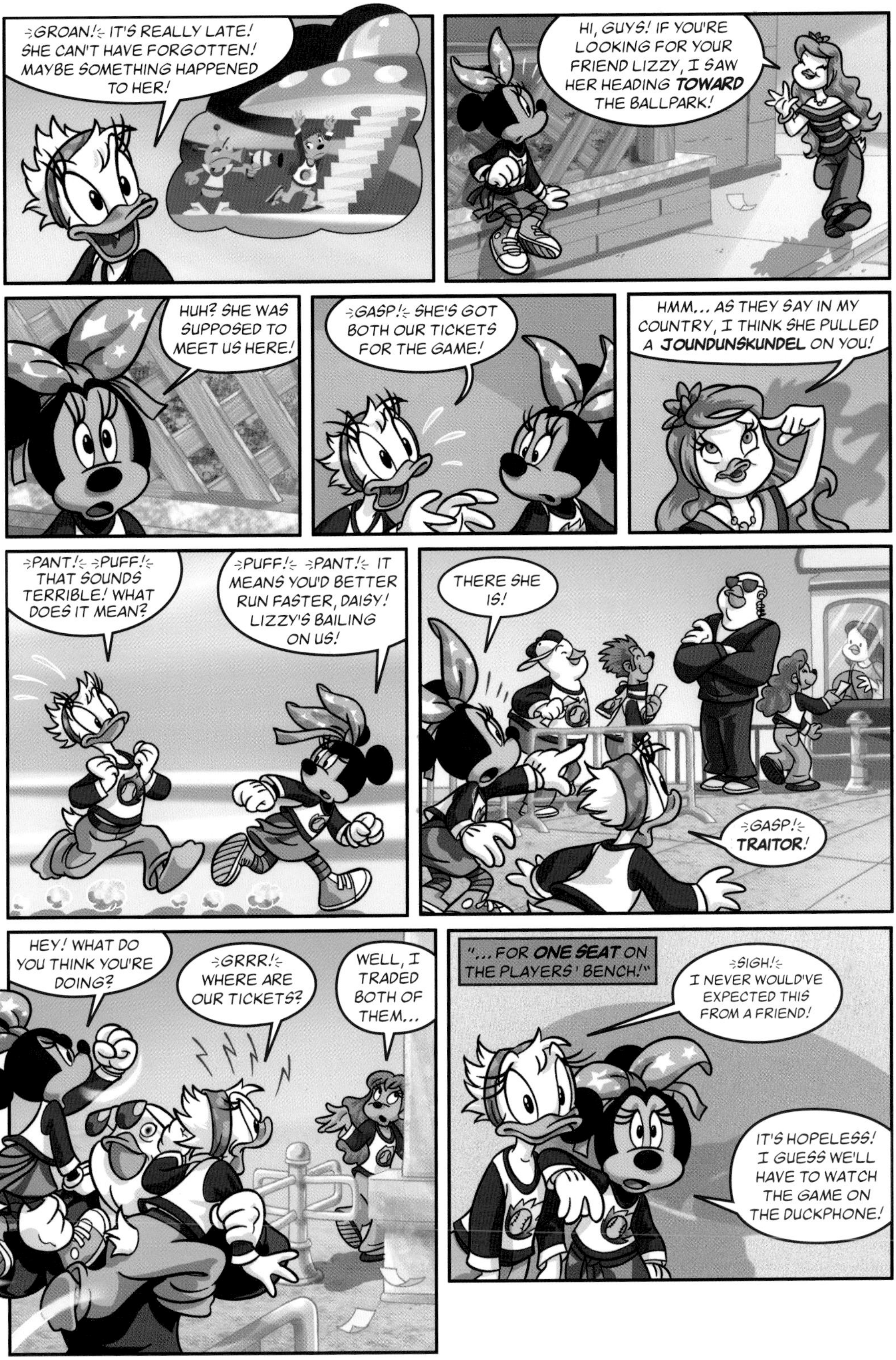

GROAN! IT'S REALLY LATE! SHE CAN'T HAVE FORGOTTEN! MAYBE SOMETHING HAPPENED TO HER!
HI, GUYS! IF YOU'RE LOOKING FOR YOUR FRIEND LIZZY, I SAW HER HEADING TOWARD THE BALLPARK!
HUH? SHE WAS SUPPOSED TO MEET US HERE!
GASP! SHE'S GOT BOTH OUR TICKETS FOR THE GAME!
HMM... AS THEY SAY IN MY COUNTRY, I THINK SHE PULLED A JOUNDUNSKUNDEL ON YOU!
PANT! PUFF! THAT SOUNDS TERRIBLE! WHAT DOES IT MEAN?
PUFF! PANT! IT MEANS YOU'D BETTER RUN FASTER, DAISY! LIZZY'S BAILING ON US!
THERE SHE IS!
GASP! TRAITOR!
HEY! WHAT DO YOU THINK YOU'RE DOING?
GRRR! WHERE ARE OUR TICKETS?
WELL, I TRADED BOTH OF THEM...
"...FOR ONE SEAT ON THE PLAYERS' BENCH!"
SIGH! I NEVER WOULD'VE EXPECTED THIS FROM A FRIEND!
IT'S HOPELESS! I GUESS WE'LL HAVE TO WATCH THE GAME ON THE DUCKPHONE!

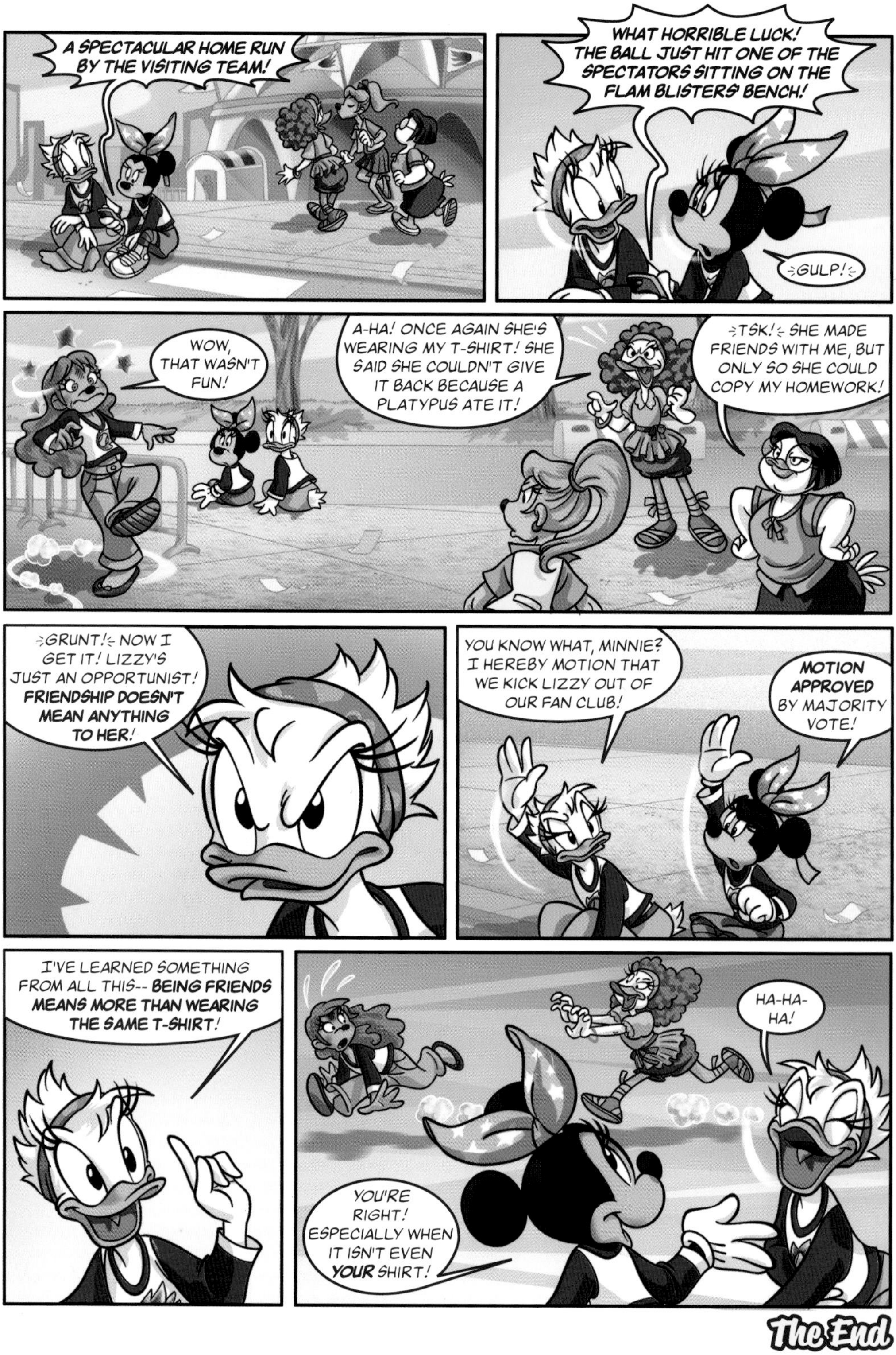
A SPECTACULAR HOME RUN BY THE VISITING TEAM!
WHAT HORRIBLE LUCK! THE BALL JUST HIT ONE OF THE SPECTATORS SITTING ON THE FLAM BLISTERS' BENCH!
GULP!
WOW, THAT WASN'T FUN!
A-HA! ONCE AGAIN SHE'S WEARING MY T-SHIRT! SHE SAID SHE COULDN'T GIVE IT BACK BECAUSE A PLATYPUS ATE IT!
TSK! SHE MADE FRIENDS WITH ME, BUT ONLY SO SHE COULD COPY MY HOMEWORK!
GRUNT! NOW I GET IT! LIZZY'S JUST AN OPPORTUNIST! FRIENDSHIP DOESN'T MEAN ANYTHING TO HER!
YOU KNOW WHAT, MINNIE? I HEREBY MOTION THAT WE KICK LIZZY OUT OF OUR FAN CLUB!
MOTION APPROVED BY MAJORITY VOTE!
I'VE LEARNED SOMETHING FROM ALL THIS-- BEING FRIENDS MEANS MORE THAN WEARING THE SAME T-SHIRT!
HA-HA-HA!
YOU'RE RIGHT! ESPECIALLY WHEN IT ISN'T EVEN YOUR SHIRT!
The End

The Wheels of Fortune

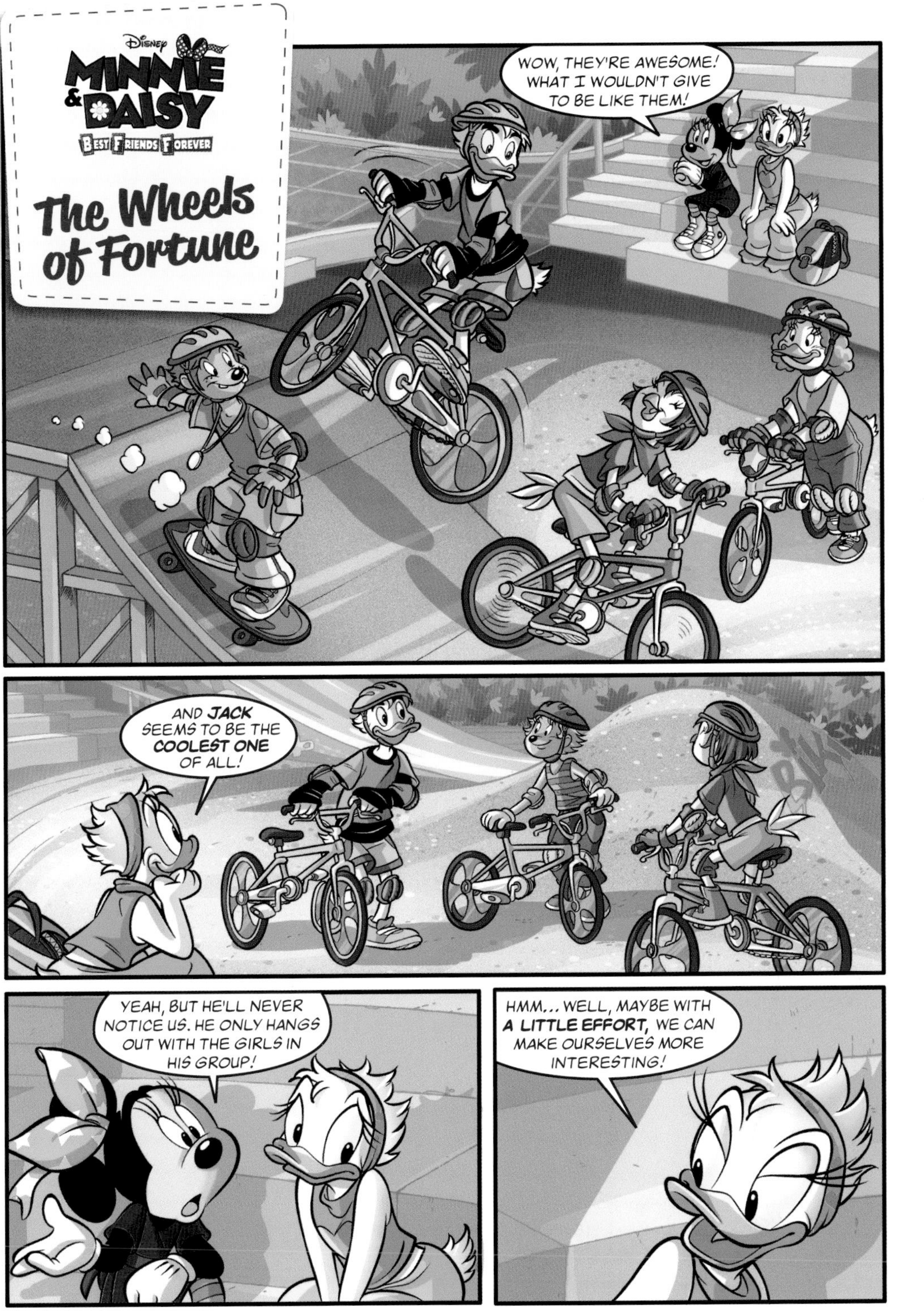

DISNEY MINNIE & DAISY BEST FRIENDS FOREVER
WOW, THEY'RE AWESOME! WHAT I WOULDN'T GIVE TO BE LIKE THEM!
AND **JACK** SEEMS TO BE THE **COOLEST ONE** OF ALL!
YEAH, BUT HE'LL NEVER NOTICE US. HE ONLY HANGS OUT WITH THE GIRLS IN HIS GROUP!
HMM... WELL, MAYBE WITH **A LITTLE EFFORT,** WE CAN MAKE OURSELVES MORE INTERESTING!

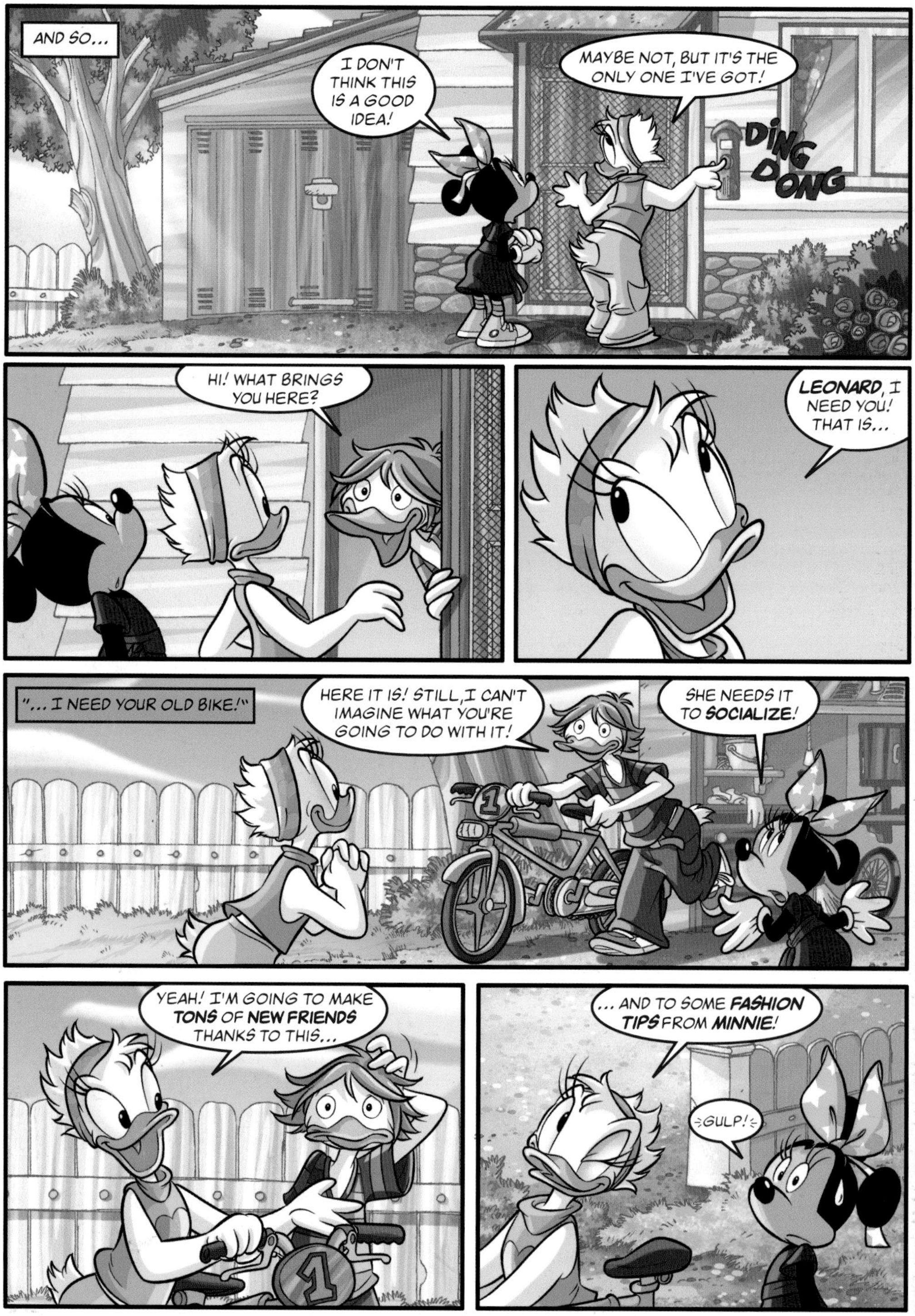
AND SO...
I DON'T THINK THIS IS A GOOD IDEA!
MAYBE NOT, BUT IT'S THE ONLY ONE I'VE GOT!
DING DONG
HI! WHAT BRINGS YOU HERE?
LEONARD, I NEED YOU! THAT IS...
"... I NEED YOUR OLD BIKE!"
HERE IT IS! STILL, I CAN'T IMAGINE WHAT YOU'RE GOING TO DO WITH IT!
SHE NEEDS IT TO SOCIALIZE!
YEAH! I'M GOING TO MAKE TONS OF NEW FRIENDS THANKS TO THIS...
... AND TO SOME FASHION TIPS FROM MINNIE!
GULP!

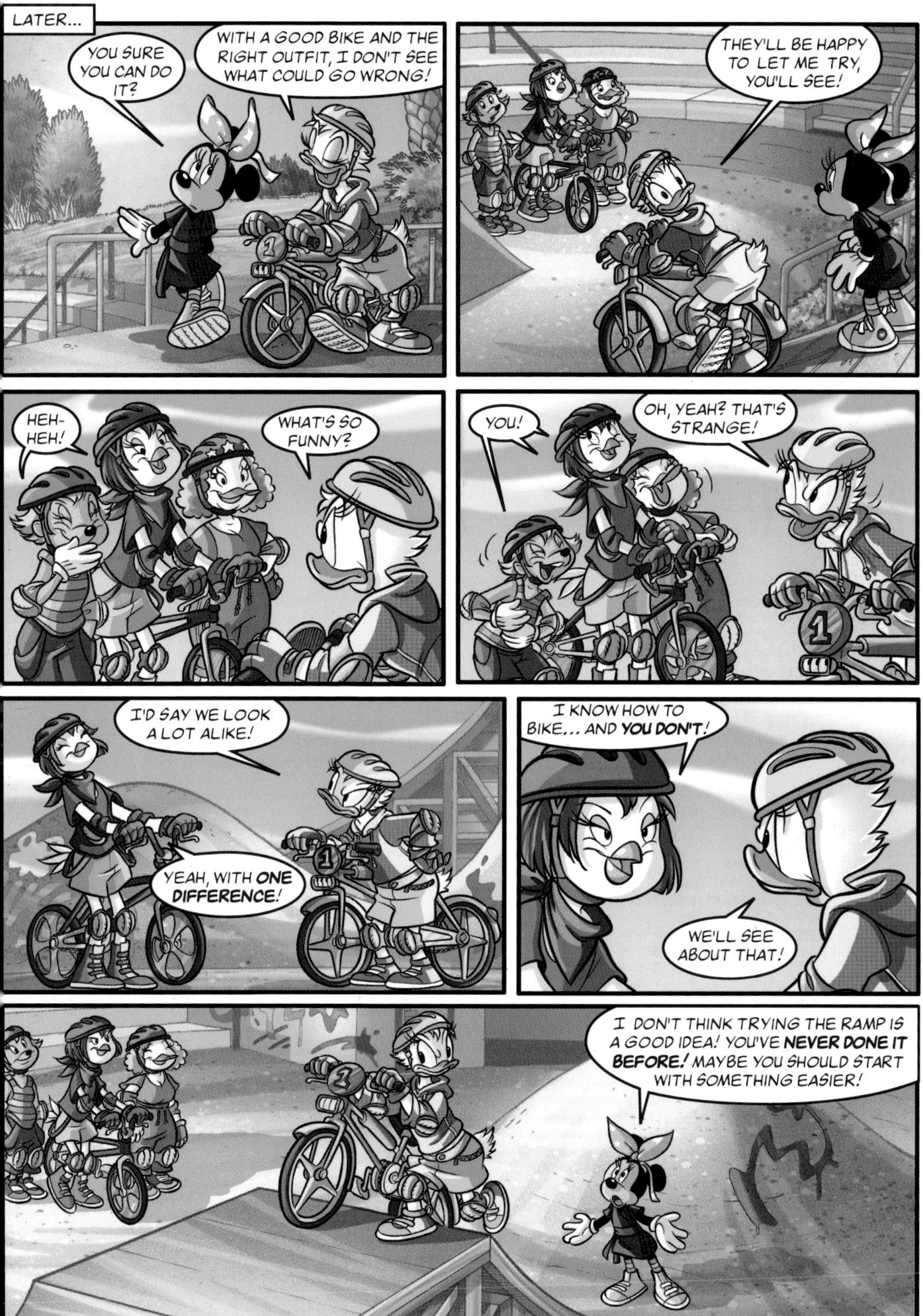
LATER...
YOU SURE YOU CAN DO IT?
WITH A GOOD BIKE AND THE RIGHT OUTFIT, I DON'T SEE WHAT COULD GO WRONG!
THEY'LL BE HAPPY TO LET ME TRY, YOU'LL SEE!
HEH-HEH!
WHAT'S SO FUNNY?
YOU!
OH, YEAH? THAT'S STRANGE!
I'D SAY WE LOOK A LOT ALIKE!
YEAH, WITH ONE DIFFERENCE!
I KNOW HOW TO BIKE... AND YOU DON'T!
WE'LL SEE ABOUT THAT!
I DON'T THINK TRYING THE RAMP IS A GOOD IDEA! YOU'VE NEVER DONE IT BEFORE! MAYBE YOU SHOULD START WITH SOMETHING EASIER!

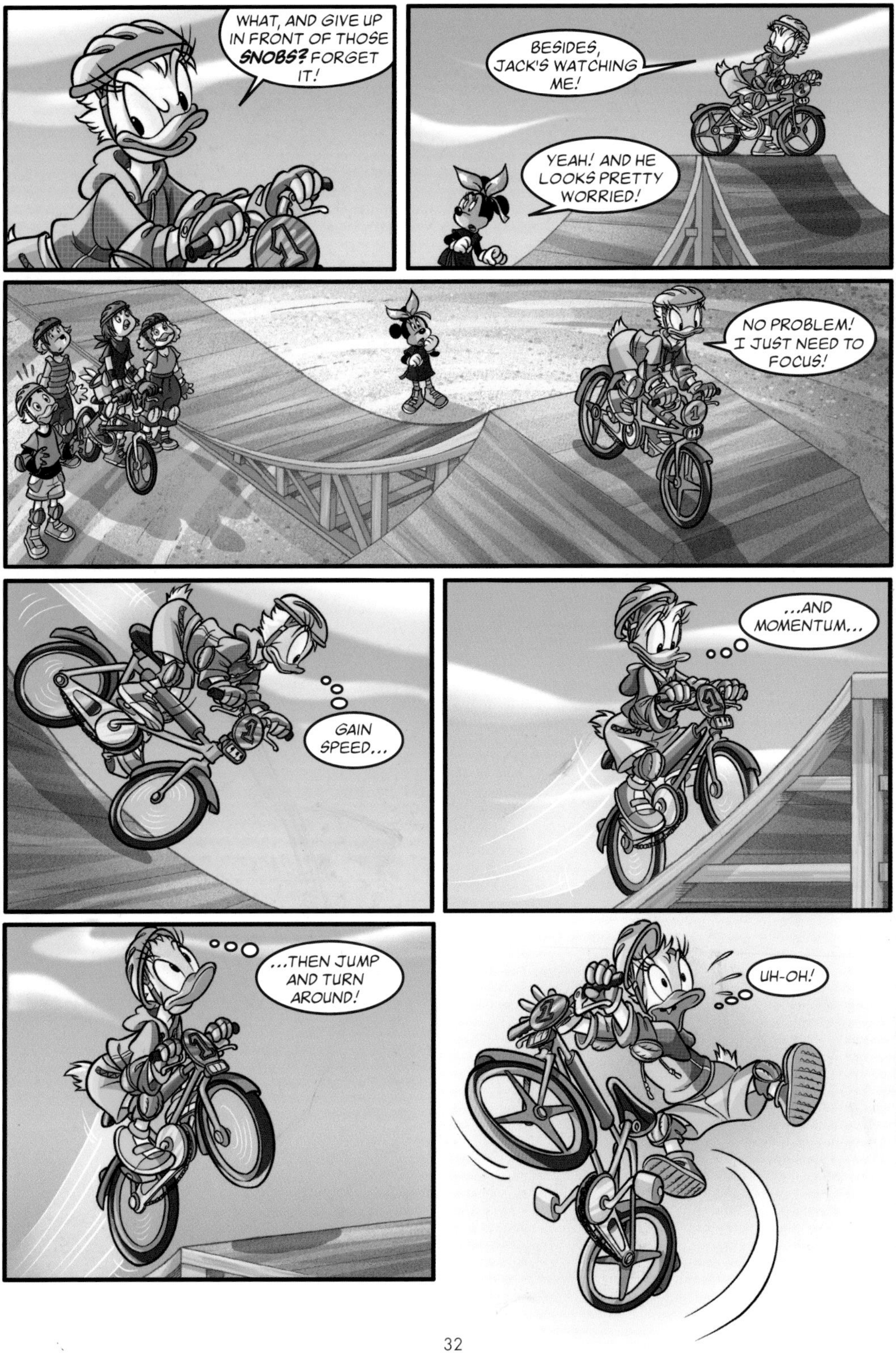
WHAT, AND GIVE UP IN FRONT OF THOSE SNOBS? FORGET IT!
BESIDES, JACK'S WATCHING ME!
YEAH! AND HE LOOKS PRETTY WORRIED!
NO PROBLEM! I JUST NEED TO FOCUS!
GAIN SPEED...
...AND MOMENTUM...
...THEN JUMP AND TURN AROUND!
UH-OH!

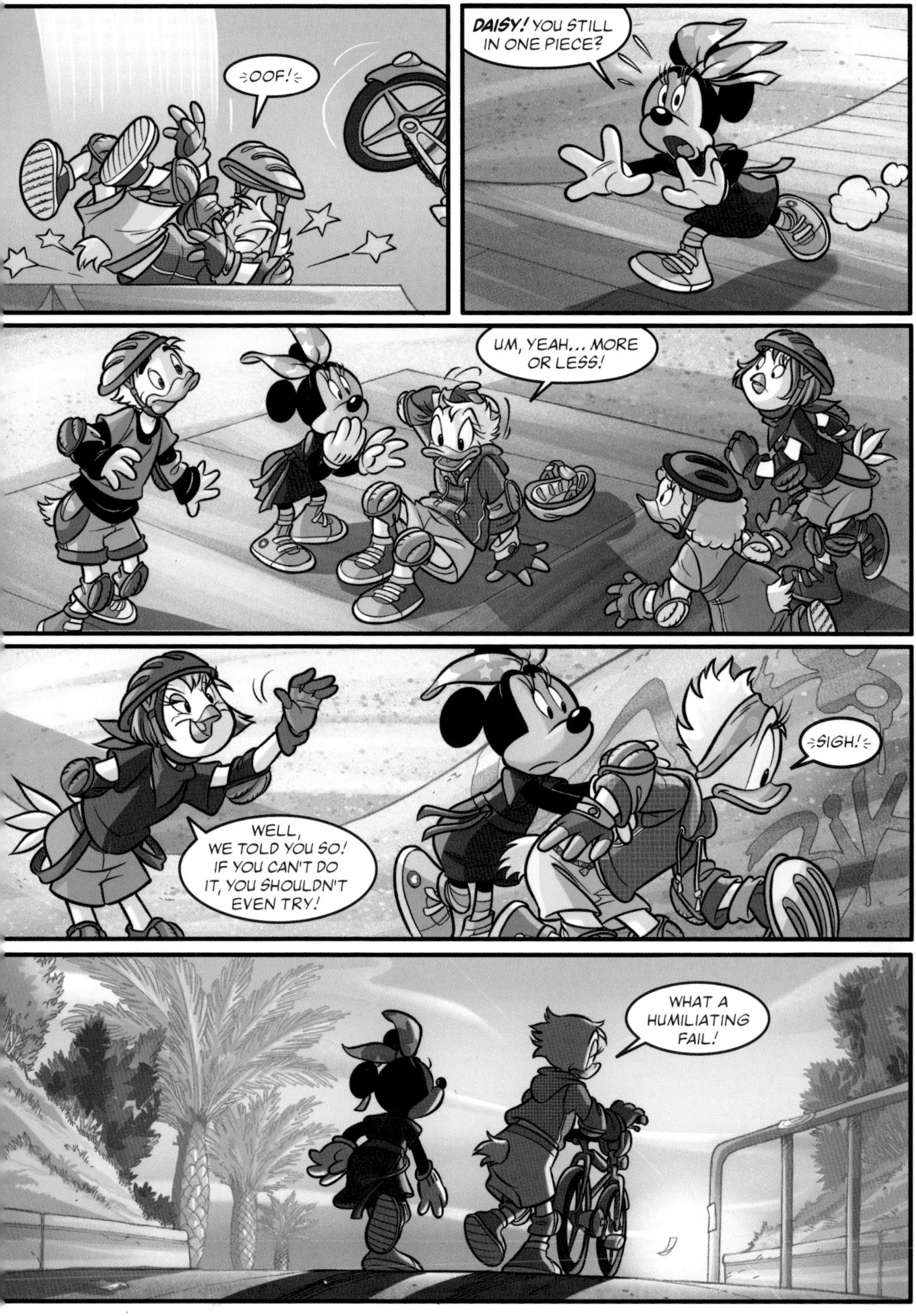
OOF!
DAISY! YOU STILL IN ONE PIECE?
UM, YEAH... MORE OR LESS!
WELL, WE TOLD YOU SO! IF YOU CAN'T DO IT, YOU SHOULDN'T EVEN TRY!
SIGH!
WHAT A HUMILIATING FAIL!

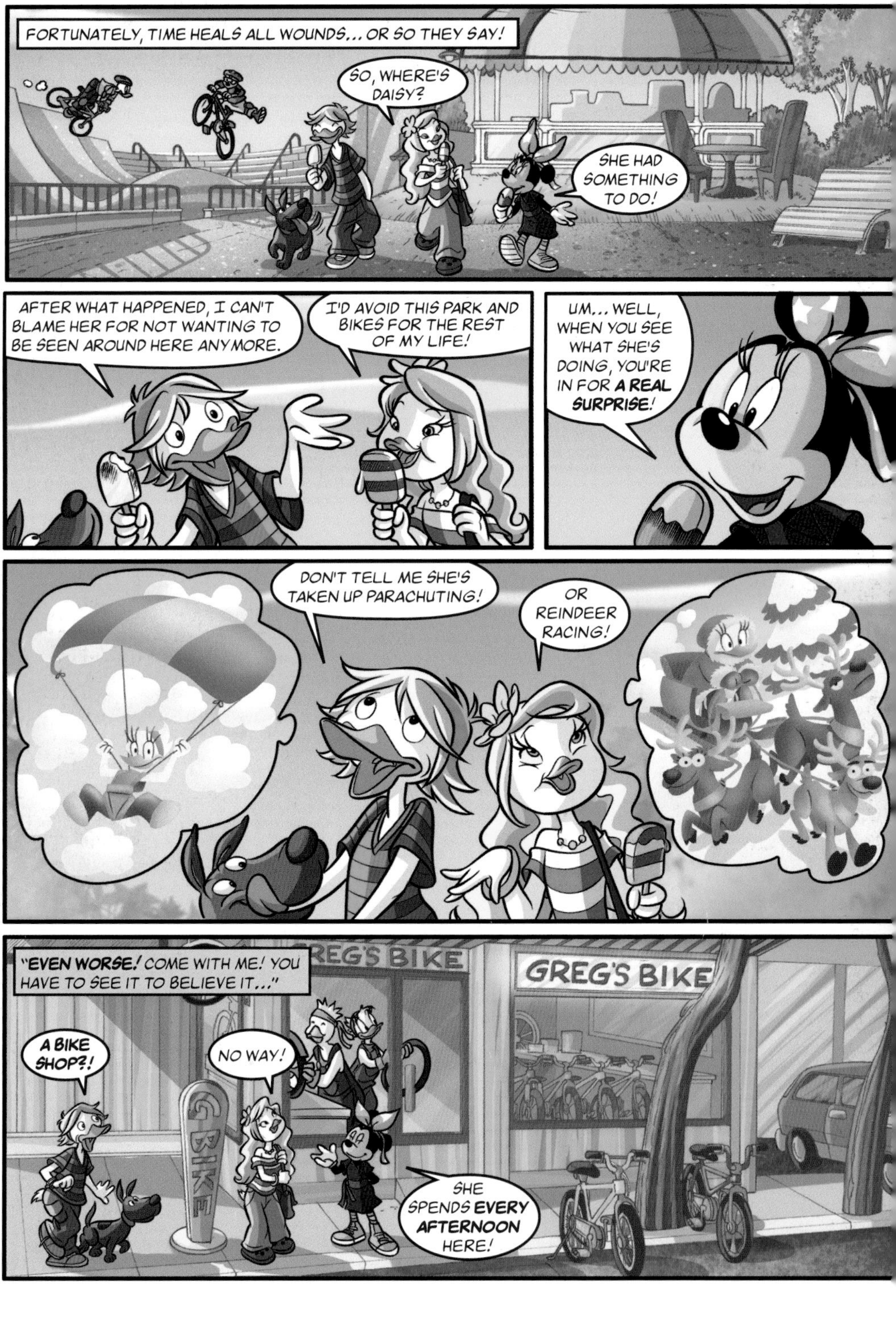
FORTUNATELY, TIME HEALS ALL WOUNDS... OR SO THEY SAY!
SO, WHERE'S DAISY?
SHE HAD SOMETHING TO DO!
AFTER WHAT HAPPENED, I CAN'T BLAME HER FOR NOT WANTING TO BE SEEN AROUND HERE ANYMORE.
I'D AVOID THIS PARK AND BIKES FOR THE REST OF MY LIFE!
UM... WELL, WHEN YOU SEE WHAT SHE'S DOING, YOU'RE IN FOR **A REAL SURPRISE**!
DON'T TELL ME SHE'S TAKEN UP PARACHUTING!
OR REINDEER RACING!
"**EVEN WORSE!** COME WITH ME! YOU HAVE TO SEE IT TO BELIEVE IT..."
GREG'S BIKE
GREG'S BIKE
A BIKE SHOP?!
NO WAY!
SHE SPENDS **EVERY AFTERNOON** HERE!

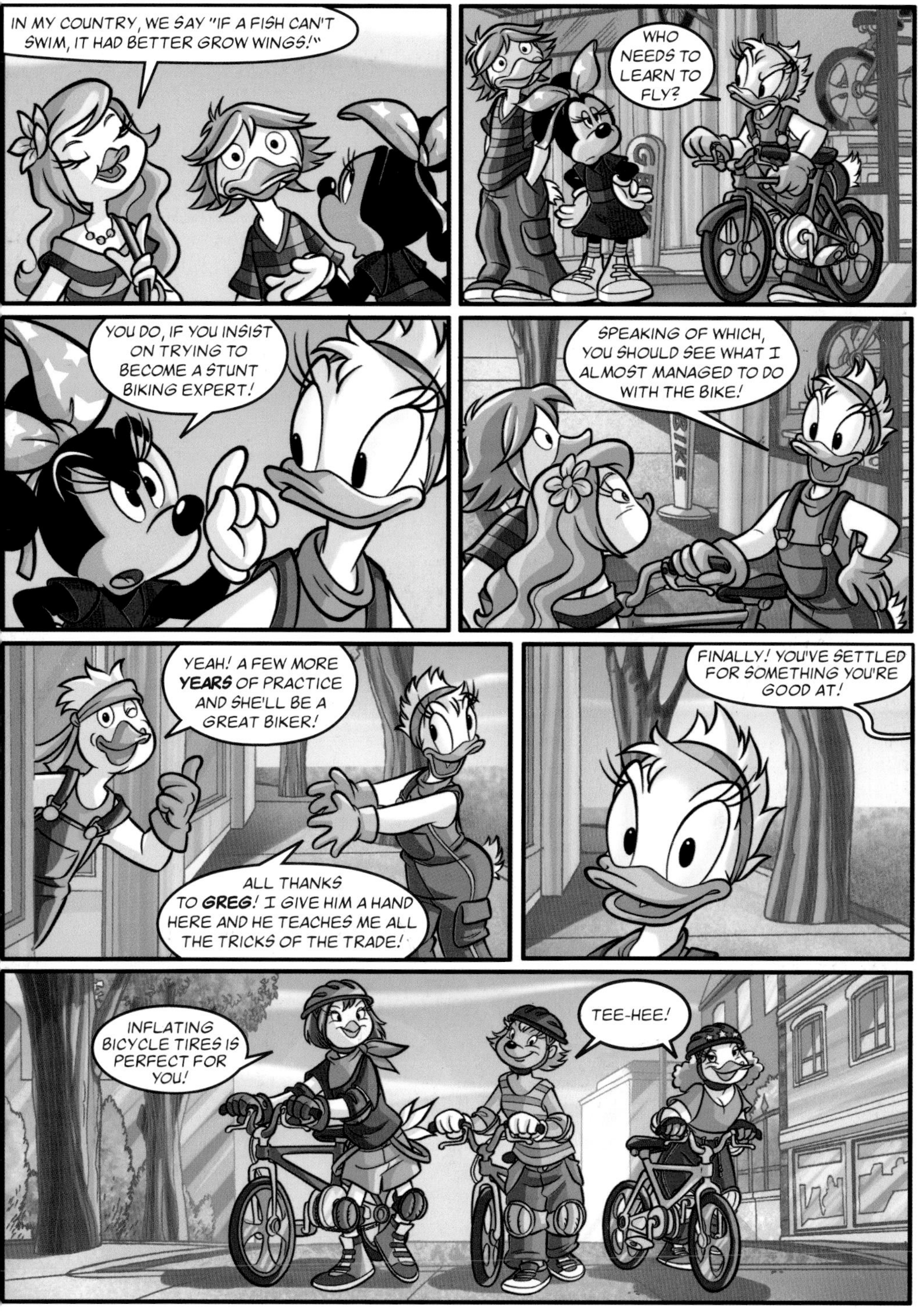
IN MY COUNTRY, WE SAY "IF A FISH CAN'T SWIM, IT HAD BETTER GROW WINGS!"
WHO NEEDS TO LEARN TO FLY?
YOU DO, IF YOU INSIST ON TRYING TO BECOME A STUNT BIKING EXPERT!
SPEAKING OF WHICH, YOU SHOULD SEE WHAT I ALMOST MANAGED TO DO WITH THE BIKE!
BIKE
YEAH! A FEW MORE **YEARS** OF PRACTICE AND SHE'LL BE A GREAT BIKER!
ALL THANKS TO **GREG**! I GIVE HIM A HAND HERE AND HE TEACHES ME ALL THE TRICKS OF THE TRADE!
FINALLY! YOU'VE SETTLED FOR SOMETHING YOU'RE GOOD AT!
INFLATING BICYCLE TIRES IS PERFECT FOR YOU!
TEE-HEE!

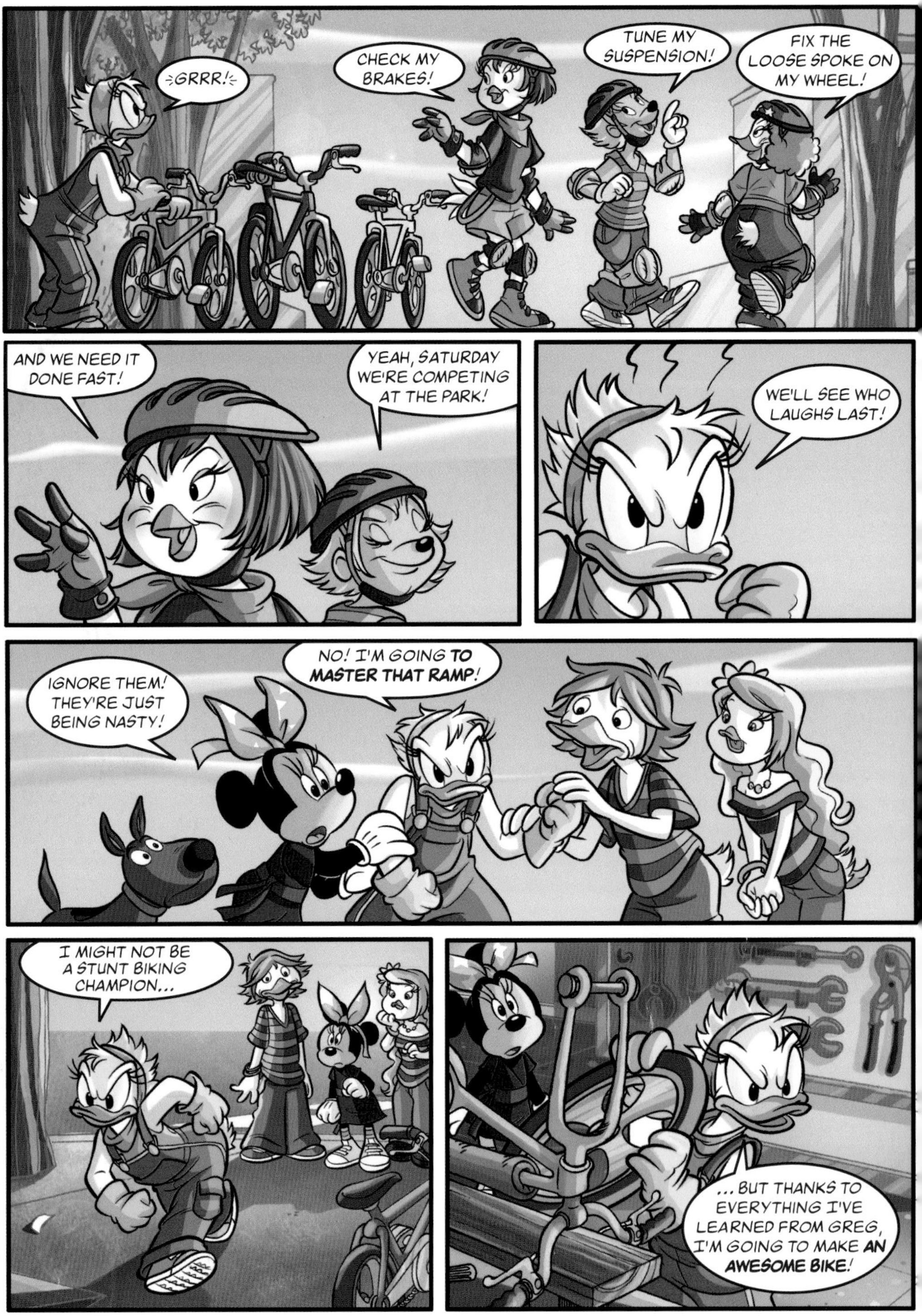
GRRR!
CHECK MY BRAKES!
TUNE MY SUSPENSION!
FIX THE LOOSE SPOKE ON MY WHEEL!
AND WE NEED IT DONE FAST!
YEAH, SATURDAY WE'RE COMPETING AT THE PARK!
WE'LL SEE WHO LAUGHS LAST!
IGNORE THEM! THEY'RE JUST BEING NASTY!
NO! I'M GOING **TO MASTER THAT RAMP**!
I MIGHT NOT BE A STUNT BIKING CHAMPION...
...BUT THANKS TO EVERYTHING I'VE LEARNED FROM GREG, I'M GOING TO MAKE **AN AWESOME BIKE**!

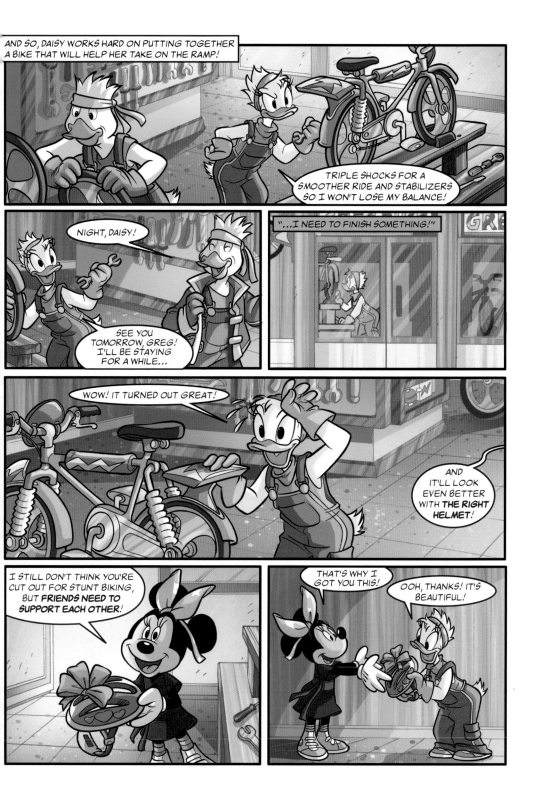

AND SO, DAISY WORKS HARD ON PUTTING TOGETHER A BIKE THAT WILL HELP HER TAKE ON THE RAMP!

TRIPLE SHOCKS FOR A SMOOTHER RIDE AND STABILIZERS SO I WON'T LOSE MY BALANCE!

NIGHT, DAISY!

SEE YOU TOMORROW, GREG! I'LL BE STAYING FOR A WHILE...

"...I NEED TO FINISH SOMETHING!"

WOW! IT TURNED OUT GREAT!

AND IT'LL LOOK EVEN BETTER WITH THE RIGHT HELMET!

I STILL DON'T THINK YOU'RE CUT OUT FOR STUNT BIKING, BUT FRIENDS NEED TO SUPPORT EACH OTHER!

THAT'S WHY I GOT YOU THIS!

OOH, THANKS! IT'S BEAUTIFUL!

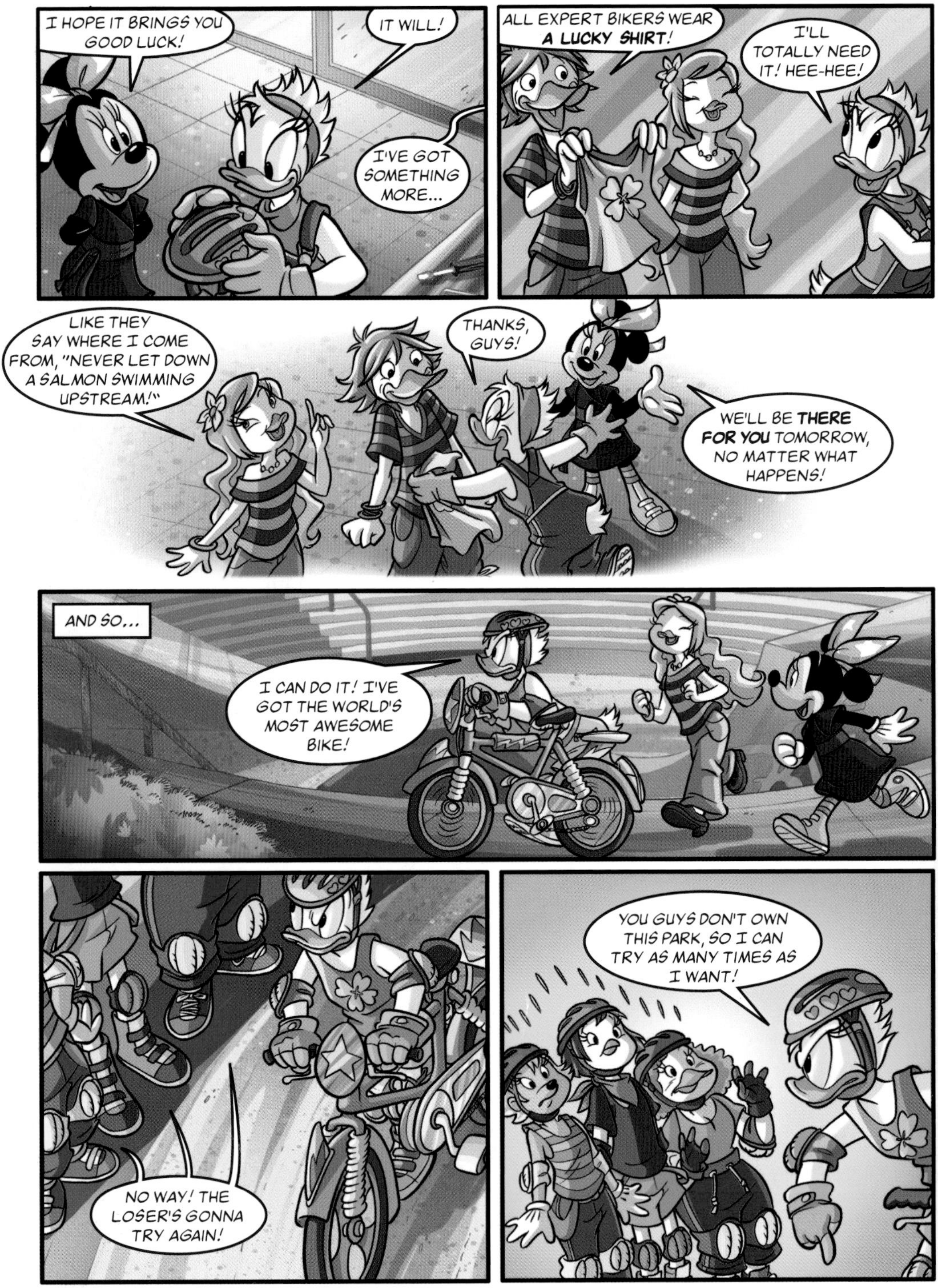
I HOPE IT BRINGS YOU GOOD LUCK!
IT WILL!
I'VE GOT SOMETHING MORE...
ALL EXPERT BIKERS WEAR **A LUCKY SHIRT**!
I'LL TOTALLY NEED IT! HEE-HEE!
LIKE THEY SAY WHERE I COME FROM, "NEVER LET DOWN A SALMON SWIMMING UPSTREAM!"
THANKS, GUYS!
WE'LL BE **THERE FOR YOU** TOMORROW, NO MATTER WHAT HAPPENS!
AND SO...
I CAN DO IT! I'VE GOT THE WORLD'S MOST AWESOME BIKE!
NO WAY! THE LOSER'S GONNA TRY AGAIN!
YOU GUYS DON'T OWN THIS PARK, SO I CAN TRY AS MANY TIMES AS I WANT!

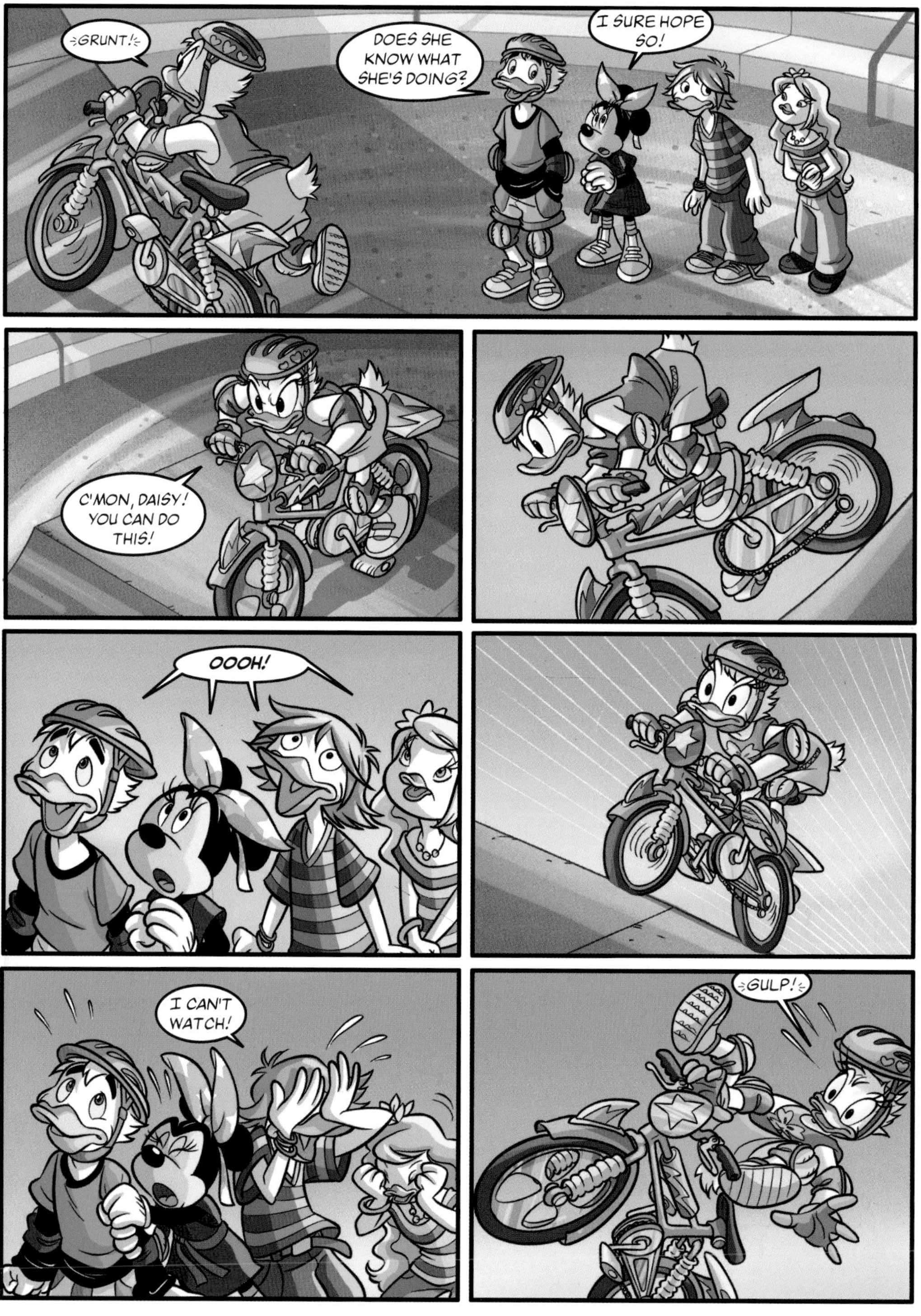
GRUNT!
DOES SHE KNOW WHAT SHE'S DOING?
I SURE HOPE SO!
C'MON, DAISY! YOU CAN DO THIS!
OOOH!
I CAN'T WATCH!
GULP!

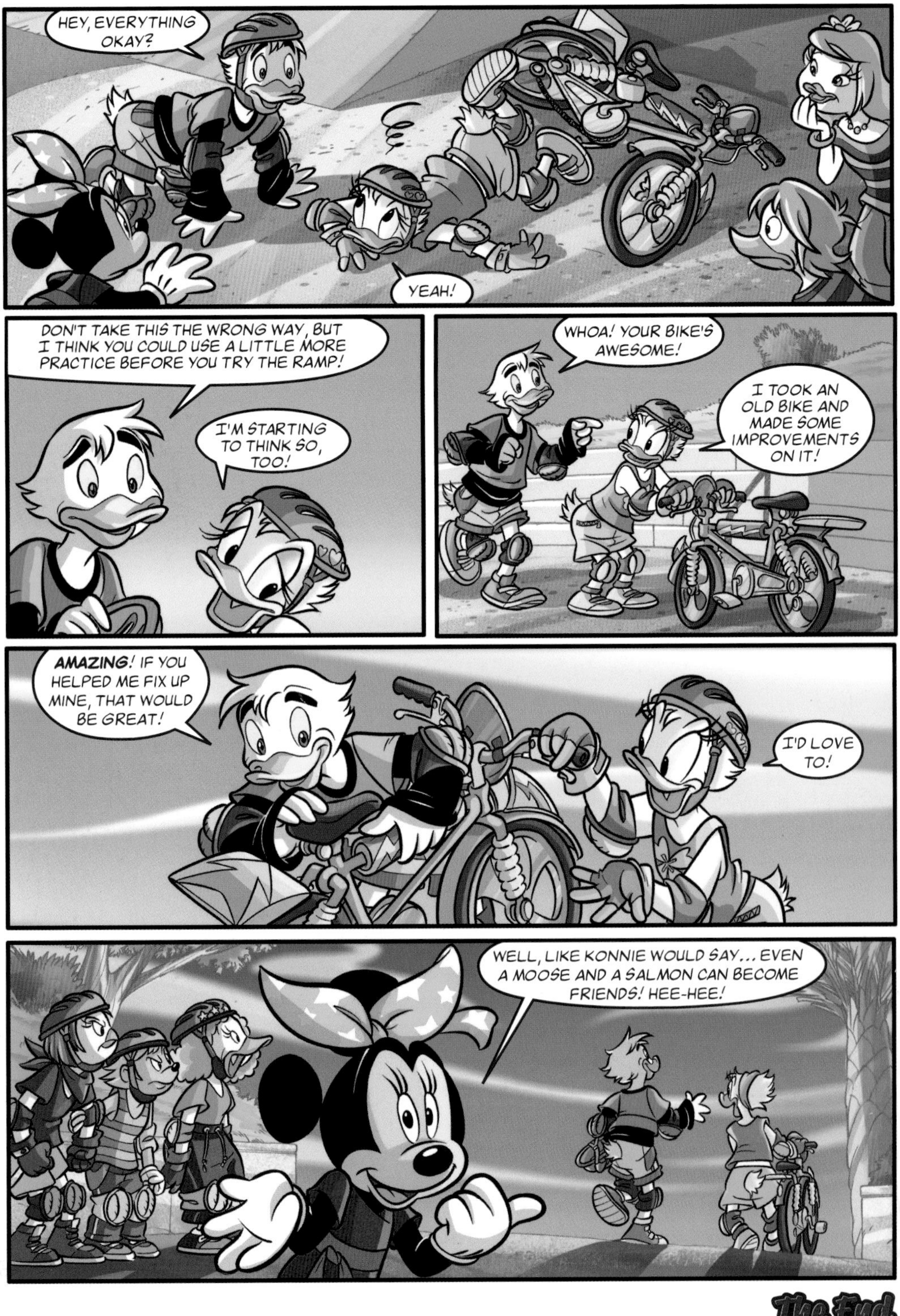
HEY, EVERYTHING OKAY?
YEAH!
DON'T TAKE THIS THE WRONG WAY, BUT I THINK YOU COULD USE A LITTLE MORE PRACTICE BEFORE YOU TRY THE RAMP!
I'M STARTING TO THINK SO, TOO!
WHOA! YOUR BIKE'S AWESOME!
I TOOK AN OLD BIKE AND MADE SOME IMPROVEMENTS ON IT!
AMAZING! IF YOU HELPED ME FIX UP MINE, THAT WOULD BE GREAT!
I'D LOVE TO!
WELL, LIKE KONNIE WOULD SAY... EVEN A MOOSE AND A SALMON CAN BECOME FRIENDS! HEE-HEE!
The End

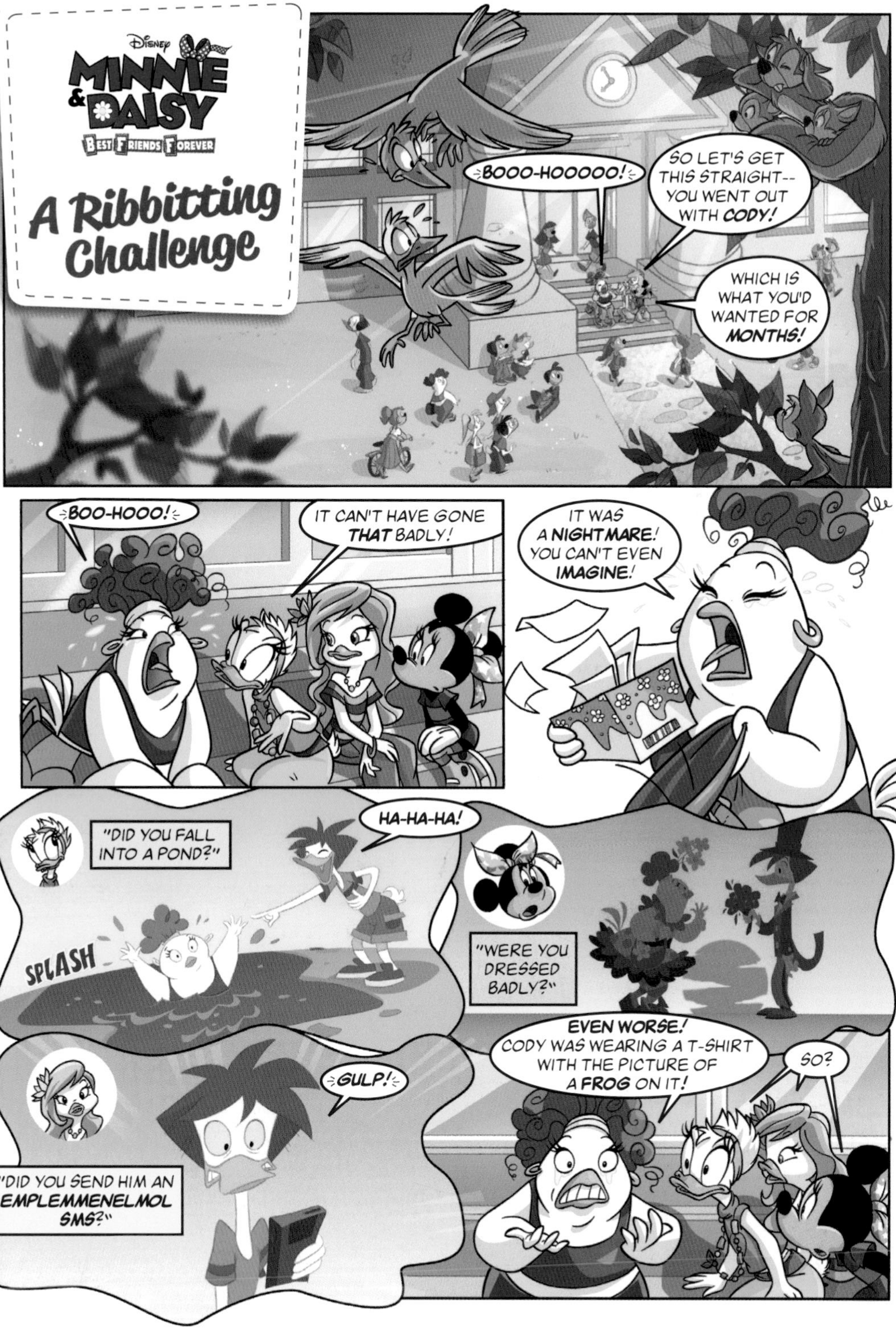
Disney
Minnie & Daisy
Best Friends Forever
A Ribbitting Challenge
BOOO-HOOOOO!
SO LET'S GET THIS STRAIGHT-- YOU WENT OUT WITH CODY!
WHICH IS WHAT YOU'D WANTED FOR MONTHS!
BOO-HOOO!
IT CAN'T HAVE GONE THAT BADLY!
IT WAS A NIGHTMARE! YOU CAN'T EVEN IMAGINE!
"DID YOU FALL INTO A POND?"
HA-HA-HA!
SPLASH
"WERE YOU DRESSED BADLY?"
GULP!
"DID YOU SEND HIM AN EMPLEMMENELMOL SMS?"
EVEN WORSE! CODY WAS WEARING A T-SHIRT WITH THE PICTURE OF A FROG ON IT!
SO?

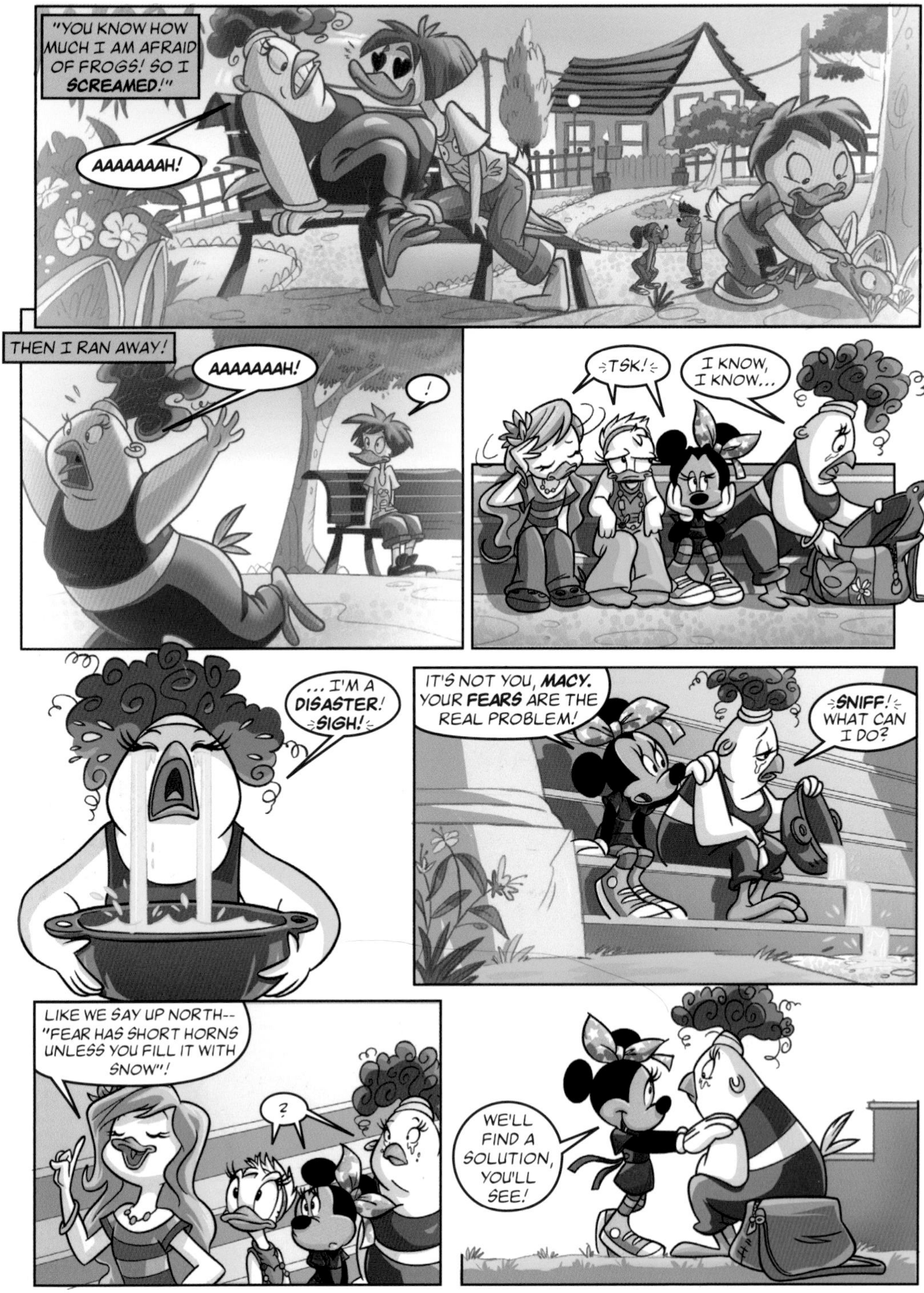
"YOU KNOW HOW MUCH I AM AFRAID OF FROGS! SO I SCREAMED!"
AAAAAAAH!
THEN I RAN AWAY!
AAAAAAAH!
!
TSK!
I KNOW, I KNOW...
...I'M A DISASTER! SIGH!
IT'S NOT YOU, MACY. YOUR FEARS ARE THE REAL PROBLEM!
SNIFF! WHAT CAN I DO?
LIKE WE SAY UP NORTH-- "FEAR HAS SHORT HORNS UNLESS YOU FILL IT WITH SNOW"!
?
WE'LL FIND A SOLUTION, YOU'LL SEE!

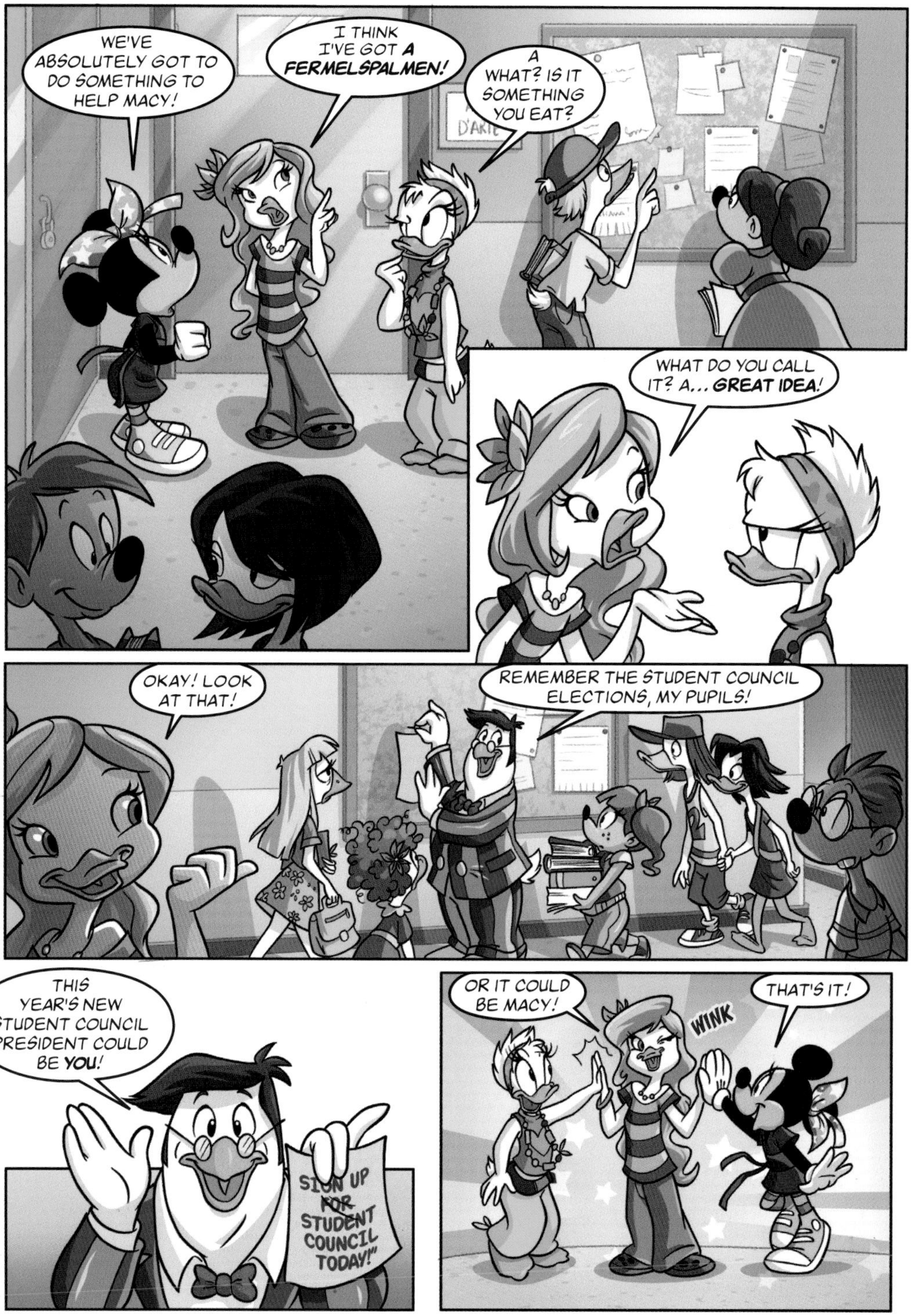
WE'VE ABSOLUTELY GOT TO DO SOMETHING TO HELP MACY!
I THINK I'VE GOT **A FERMELSPALMEN!**
A WHAT? IS IT SOMETHING YOU EAT?
WHAT DO YOU CALL IT? A... **GREAT IDEA!**
OKAY! LOOK AT THAT!
REMEMBER THE STUDENT COUNCIL ELECTIONS, MY PUPILS!
THIS YEAR'S NEW STUDENT COUNCIL PRESIDENT COULD BE **YOU!**
SIGN UP FOR STUDENT COUNCIL TODAY!"
OR IT COULD BE MACY!
WINK
THAT'S IT!

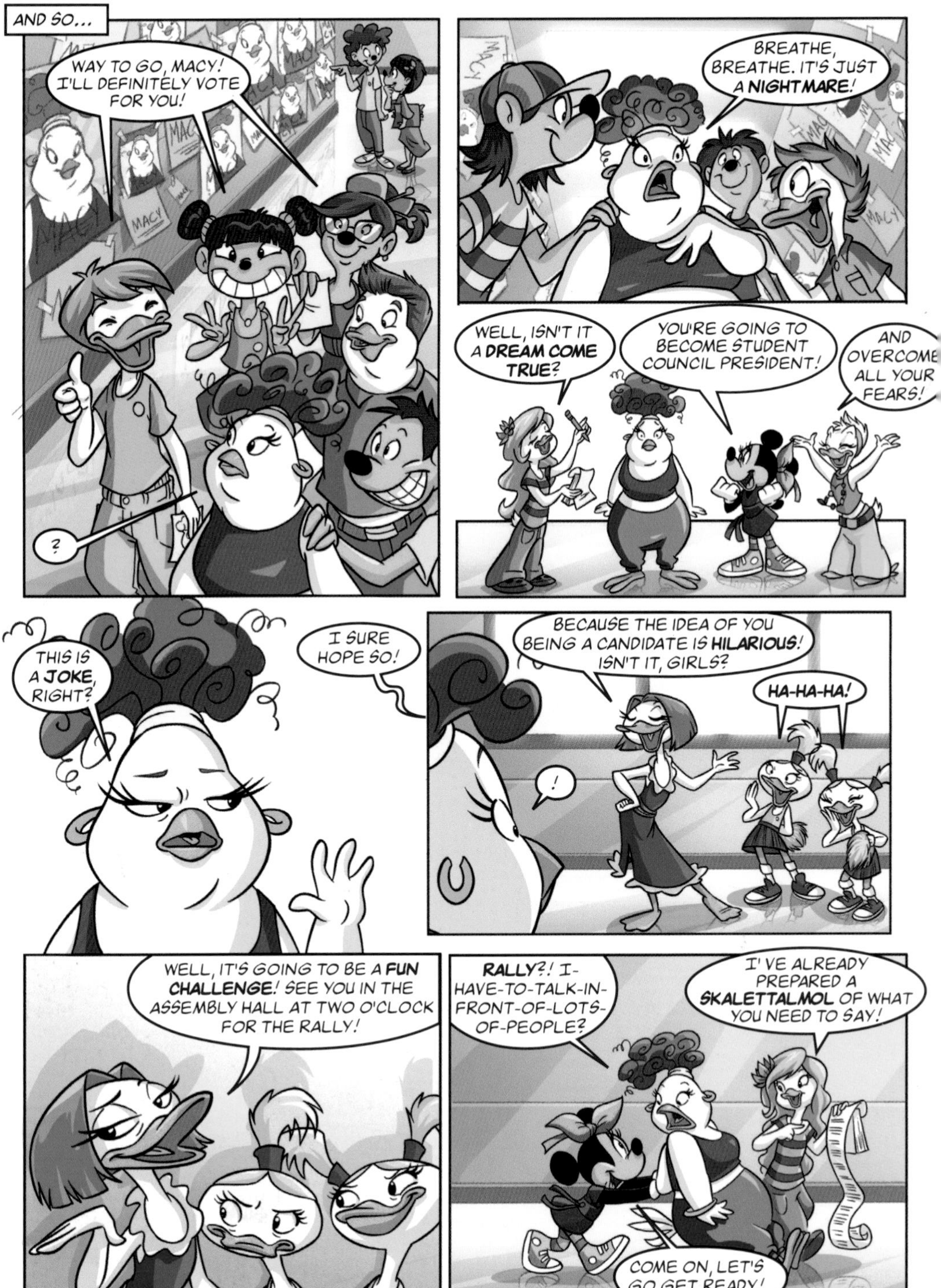
AND SO...
WAY TO GO, MACY! I'LL DEFINITELY VOTE FOR YOU!
?
BREATHE, BREATHE. IT'S JUST A NIGHTMARE!
WELL, ISN'T IT A DREAM COME TRUE?
YOU'RE GOING TO BECOME STUDENT COUNCIL PRESIDENT!
AND OVERCOME ALL YOUR FEARS!
THIS IS A JOKE, RIGHT?
I SURE HOPE SO!
BECAUSE THE IDEA OF YOU BEING A CANDIDATE IS HILARIOUS! ISN'T IT, GIRLS?
HA-HA-HA!
!
WELL, IT'S GOING TO BE A FUN CHALLENGE! SEE YOU IN THE ASSEMBLY HALL AT TWO O'CLOCK FOR THE RALLY!
RALLY?! I-HAVE-TO-TALK-IN-FRONT-OF-LOTS-OF-PEOPLE?
I'VE ALREADY PREPARED A SKALETTALMOL OF WHAT YOU NEED TO SAY!
COME ON, LET'S GO GET READY!

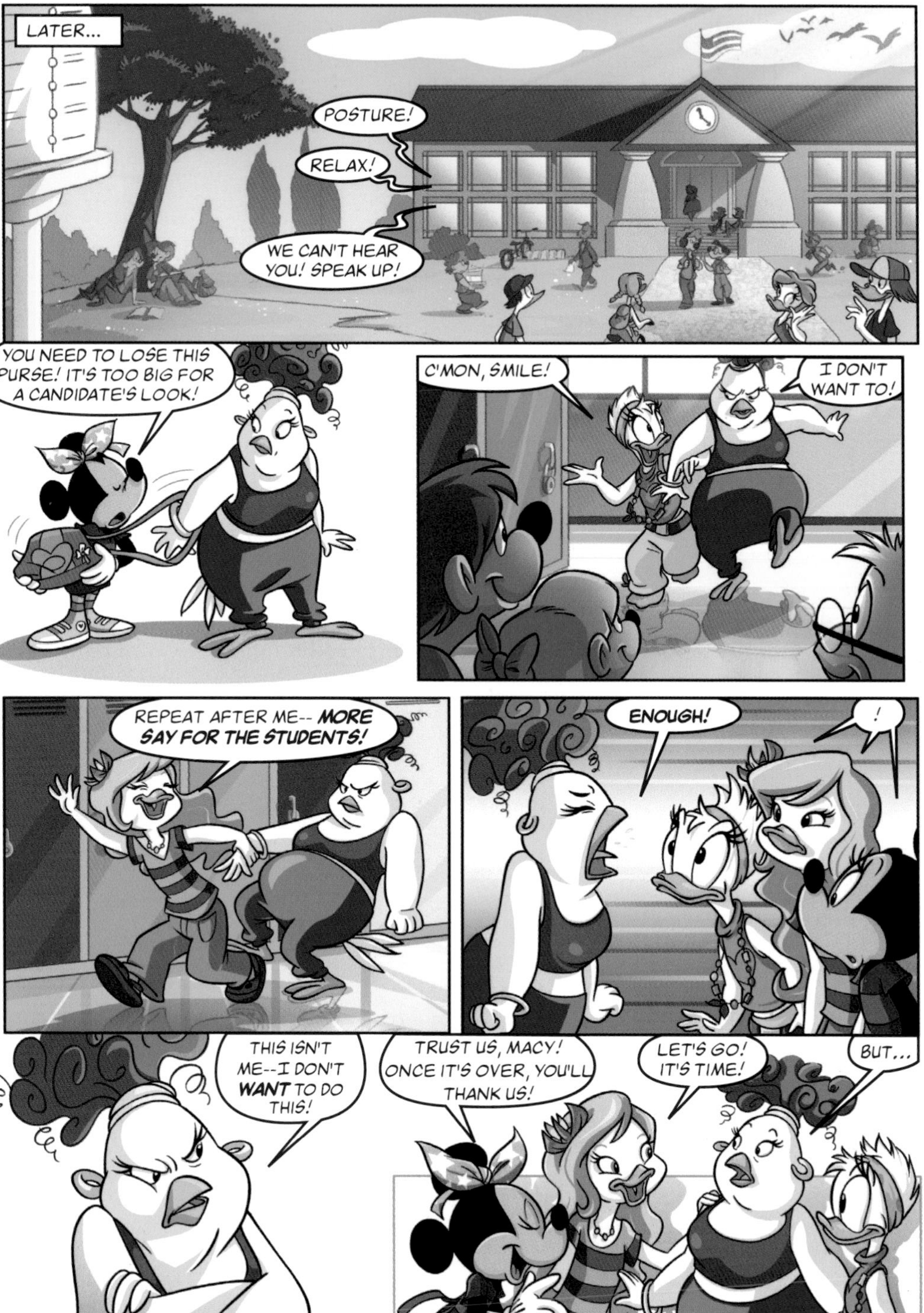
LATER...
POSTURE!
RELAX!
WE CAN'T HEAR YOU! SPEAK UP!
YOU NEED TO LOSE THIS PURSE! IT'S TOO BIG FOR A CANDIDATE'S LOOK!
C'MON, SMILE!
I DON'T WANT TO!
REPEAT AFTER ME-- MORE SAY FOR THE STUDENTS!
ENOUGH!
!
THIS ISN'T ME--I DON'T WANT TO DO THIS!
TRUST US, MACY! ONCE IT'S OVER, YOU'LL THANK US!
LET'S GO! IT'S TIME!
BUT...

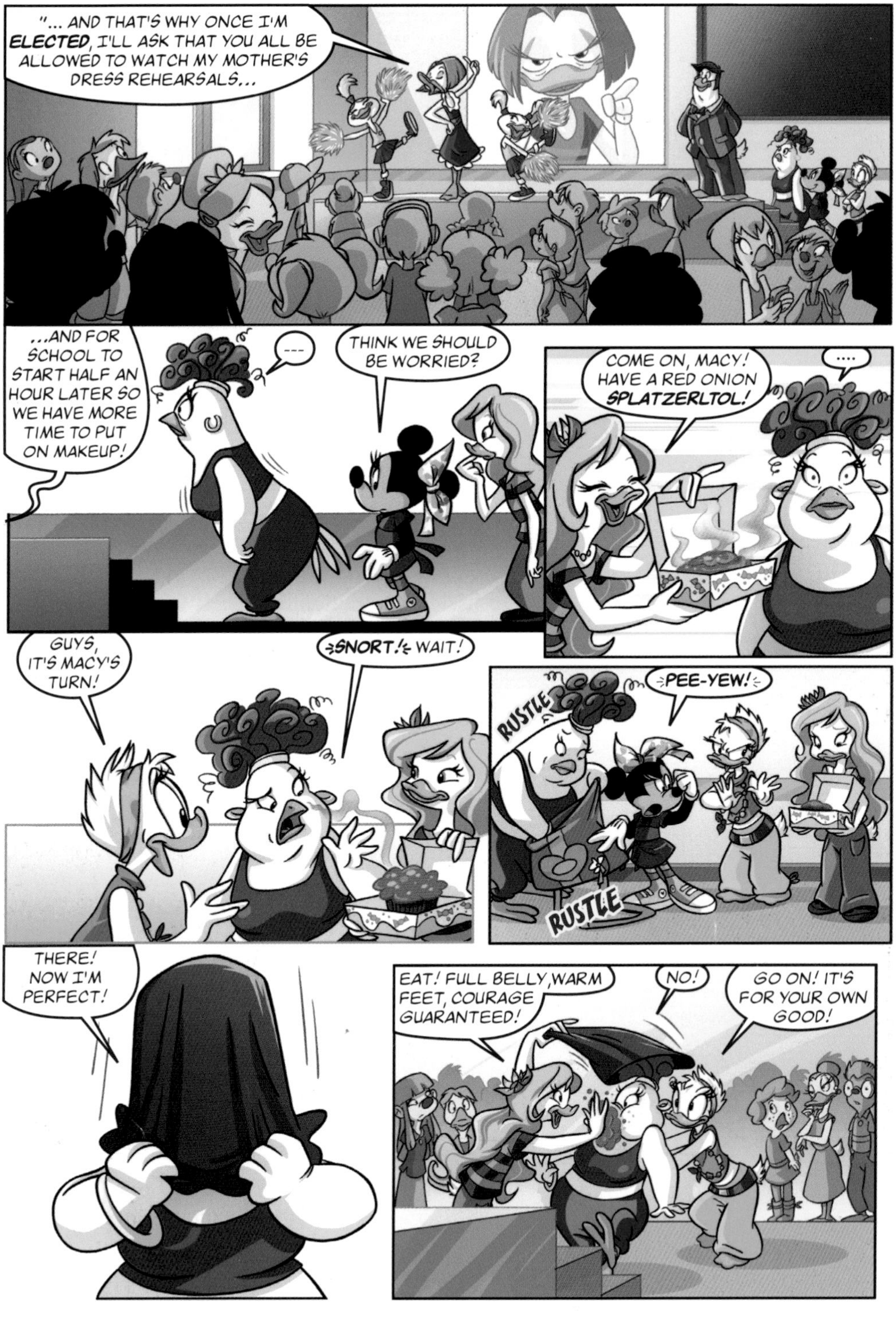
"... AND THAT'S WHY ONCE I'M ELECTED, I'LL ASK THAT YOU ALL BE ALLOWED TO WATCH MY MOTHER'S DRESS REHEARSALS...
...AND FOR SCHOOL TO START HALF AN HOUR LATER SO WE HAVE MORE TIME TO PUT ON MAKEUP!

THINK WE SHOULD BE WORRIED?
COME ON, MACY! HAVE A RED ONION SPLATZERLTOL!
....
GUYS, IT'S MACY'S TURN!
SNORT! WAIT!
RUSTLE
PEE-YEW!
RUSTLE
THERE! NOW I'M PERFECT!
EAT! FULL BELLY, WARM FEET, COURAGE GUARANTEED!
NO!
GO ON! IT'S FOR YOUR OWN GOOD!

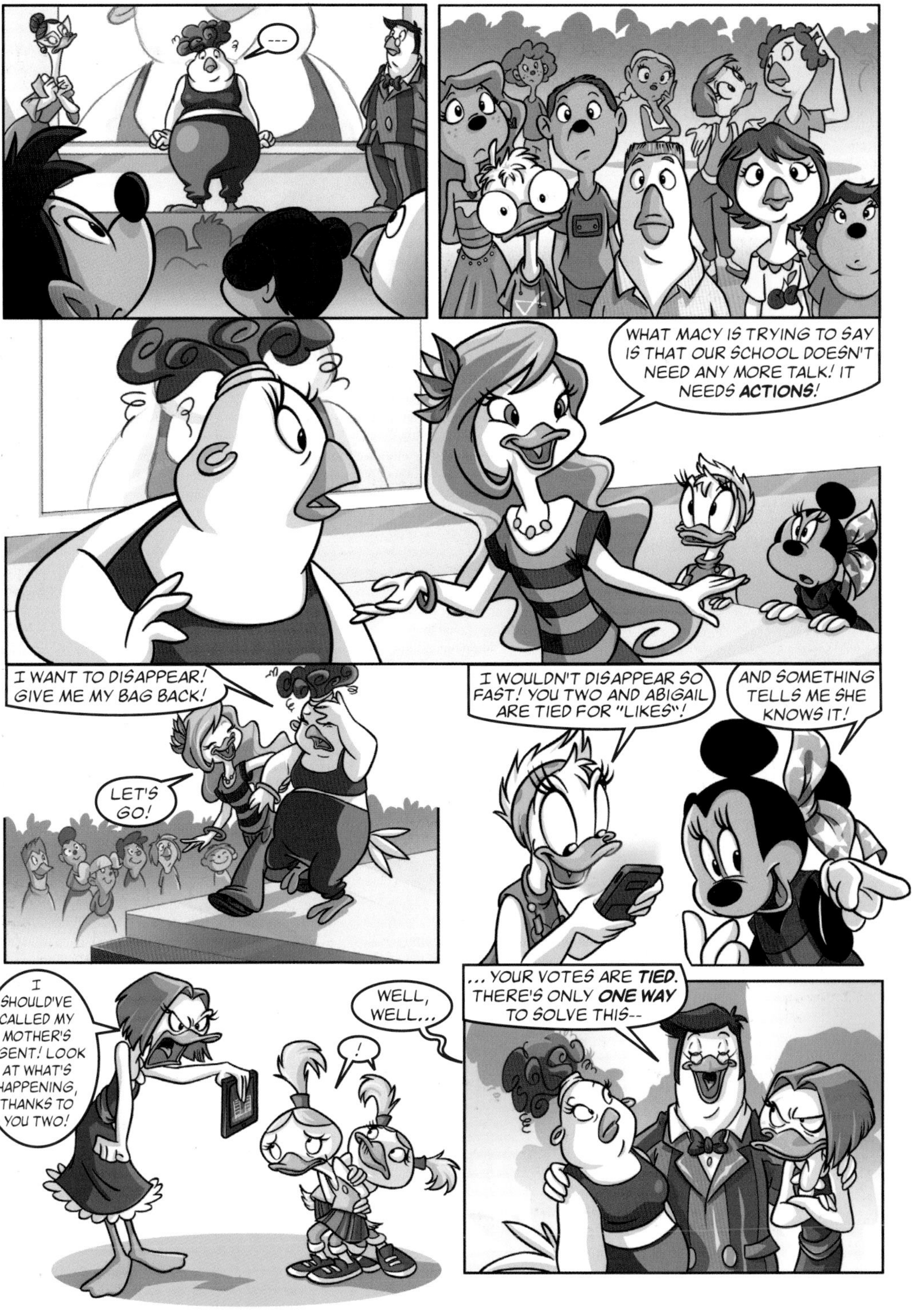

WHAT MACY IS TRYING TO SAY IS THAT OUR SCHOOL DOESN'T NEED ANY MORE TALK! IT NEEDS **ACTIONS**!
I WANT TO DISAPPEAR! GIVE ME MY BAG BACK!
LET'S GO!
I WOULDN'T DISAPPEAR SO FAST! YOU TWO AND ABIGAIL ARE TIED FOR "LIKES"!
AND SOMETHING TELLS ME SHE KNOWS IT!
I SHOULD'VE CALLED MY MOTHER'S AGENT! LOOK AT WHAT'S HAPPENING, THANKS TO YOU TWO!
!
WELL, WELL...
... YOUR VOTES ARE **TIED**. THERE'S ONLY **ONE WAY** TO SOLVE THIS--

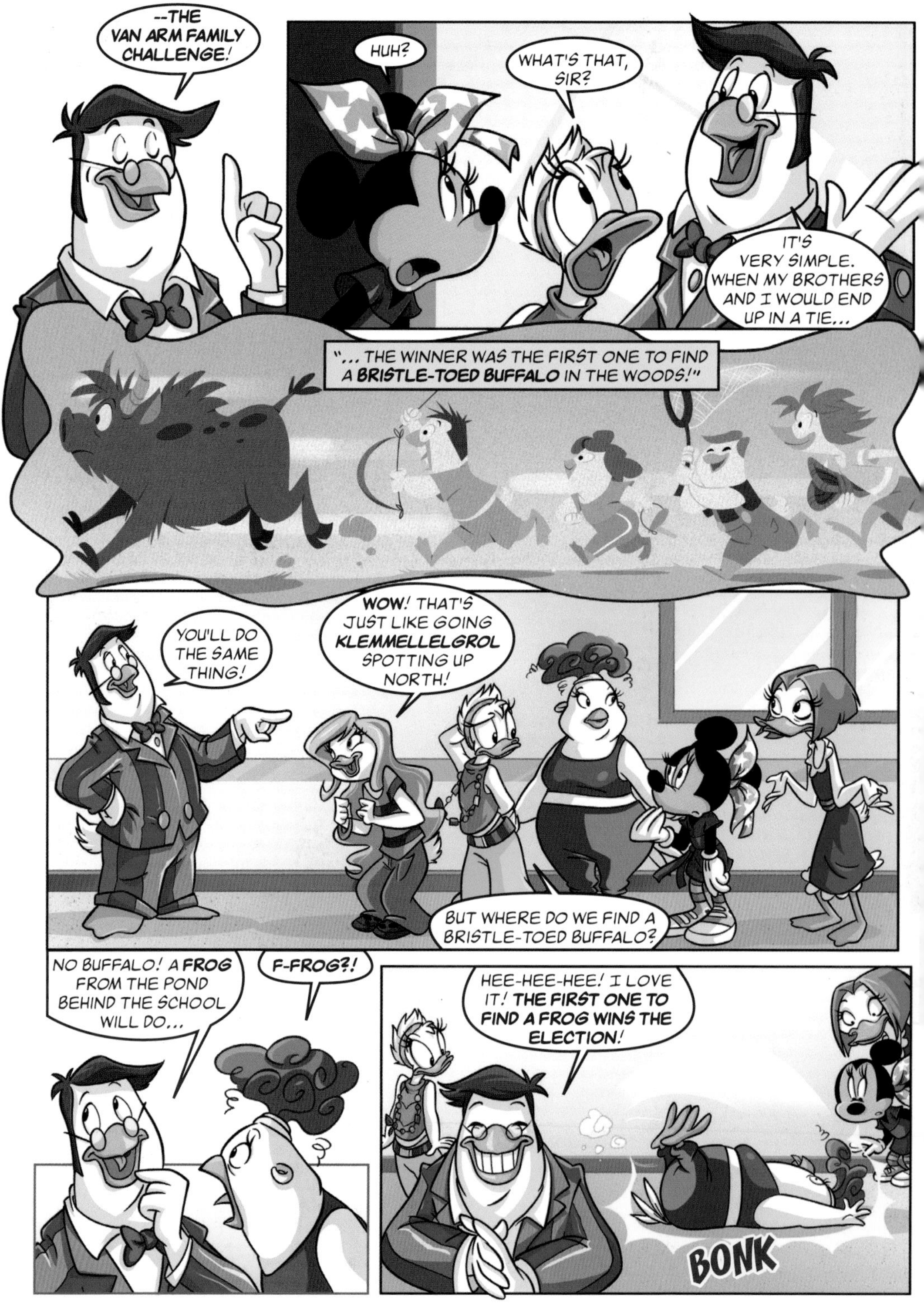
--THE VAN ARM FAMILY CHALLENGE!
HUH?
WHAT'S THAT, SIR?
IT'S VERY SIMPLE. WHEN MY BROTHERS AND I WOULD END UP IN A TIE...
"...THE WINNER WAS THE FIRST ONE TO FIND A BRISTLE-TOED BUFFALO IN THE WOODS!"
YOU'LL DO THE SAME THING!
WOW! THAT'S JUST LIKE GOING KLEMMELLELGROL SPOTTING UP NORTH!
BUT WHERE DO WE FIND A BRISTLE-TOED BUFFALO?
NO BUFFALO! A FROG FROM THE POND BEHIND THE SCHOOL WILL DO...
F-FROG?!
HEE-HEE-HEE! I LOVE IT! THE FIRST ONE TO FIND A FROG WINS THE ELECTION!
BONK

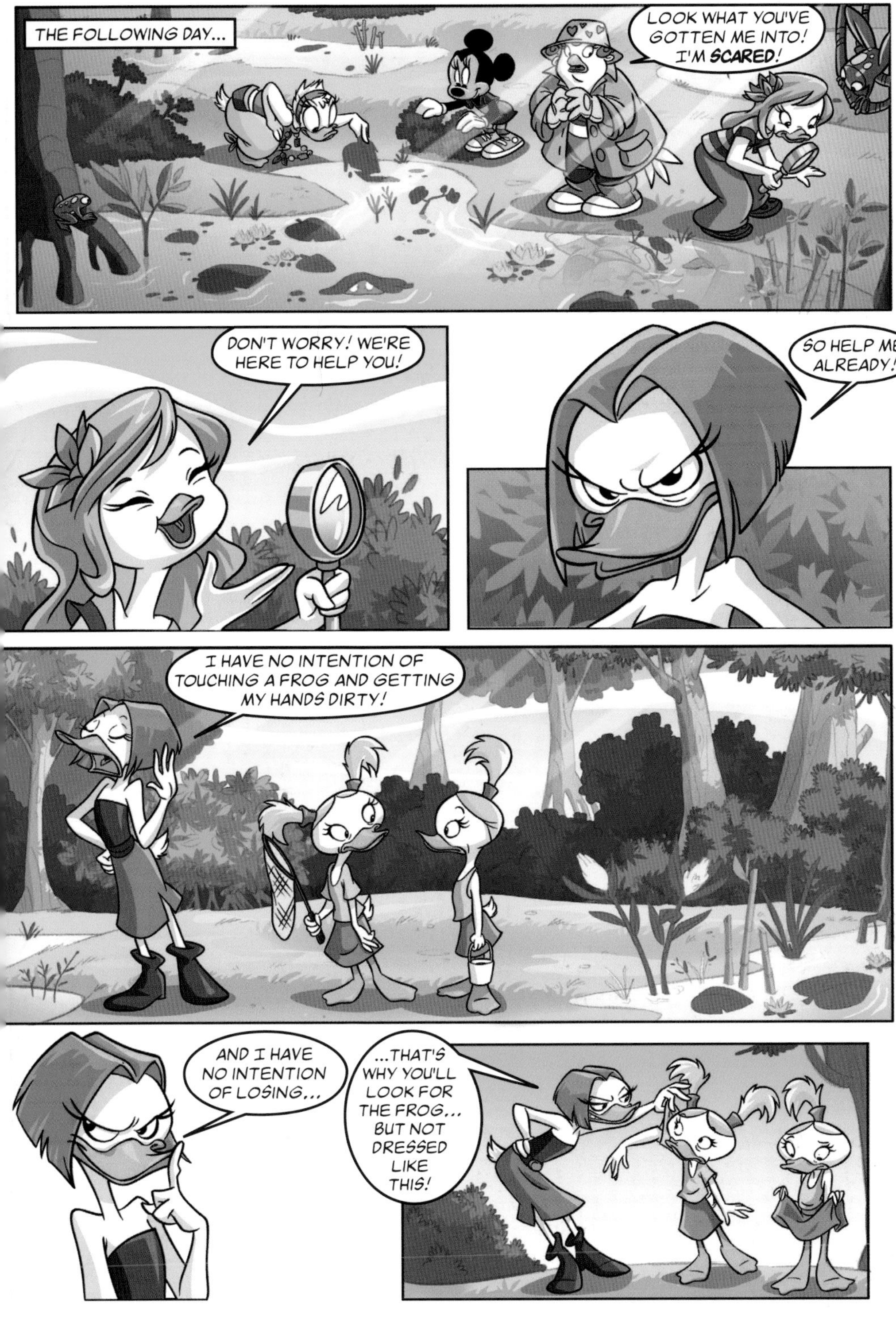
THE FOLLOWING DAY...
LOOK WHAT YOU'VE GOTTEN ME INTO! I'M SCARED!
DON'T WORRY! WE'RE HERE TO HELP YOU!
SO HELP ME, ALREADY!
I HAVE NO INTENTION OF TOUCHING A FROG AND GETTING MY HANDS DIRTY!
AND I HAVE NO INTENTION OF LOSING,...
...THAT'S WHY YOU'LL LOOK FOR THE FROG... BUT NOT DRESSED LIKE THIS!

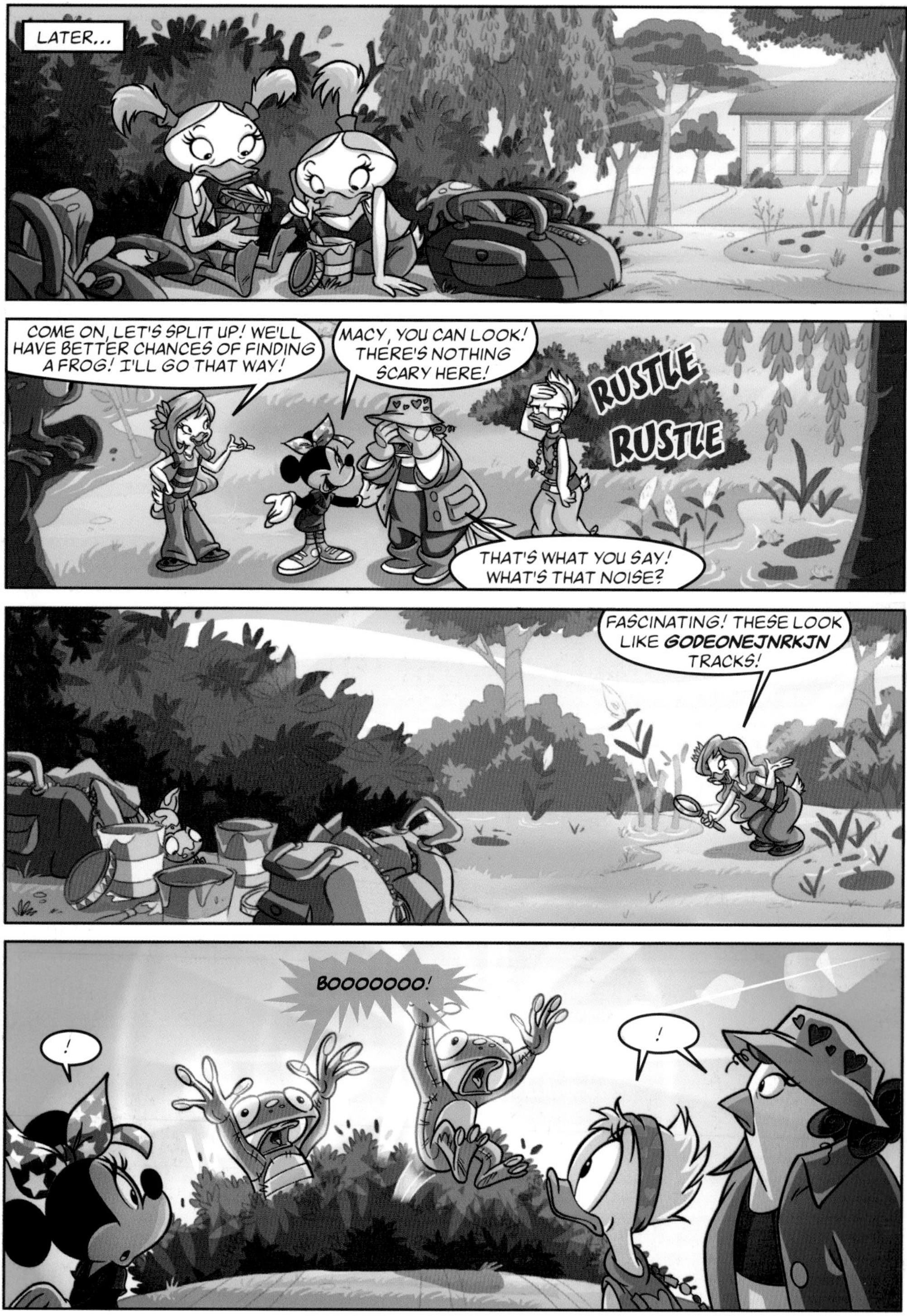
LATER...
COME ON, LET'S SPLIT UP! WE'LL HAVE BETTER CHANCES OF FINDING A FROG! I'LL GO THAT WAY!
MACY, YOU CAN LOOK! THERE'S NOTHING SCARY HERE!
RUSTLE
RUSTLE
THAT'S WHAT YOU SAY! WHAT'S THAT NOISE?
FASCINATING! THESE LOOK LIKE **GODEONEJNRKJN** TRACKS!
BOOOOOOO!
!
!

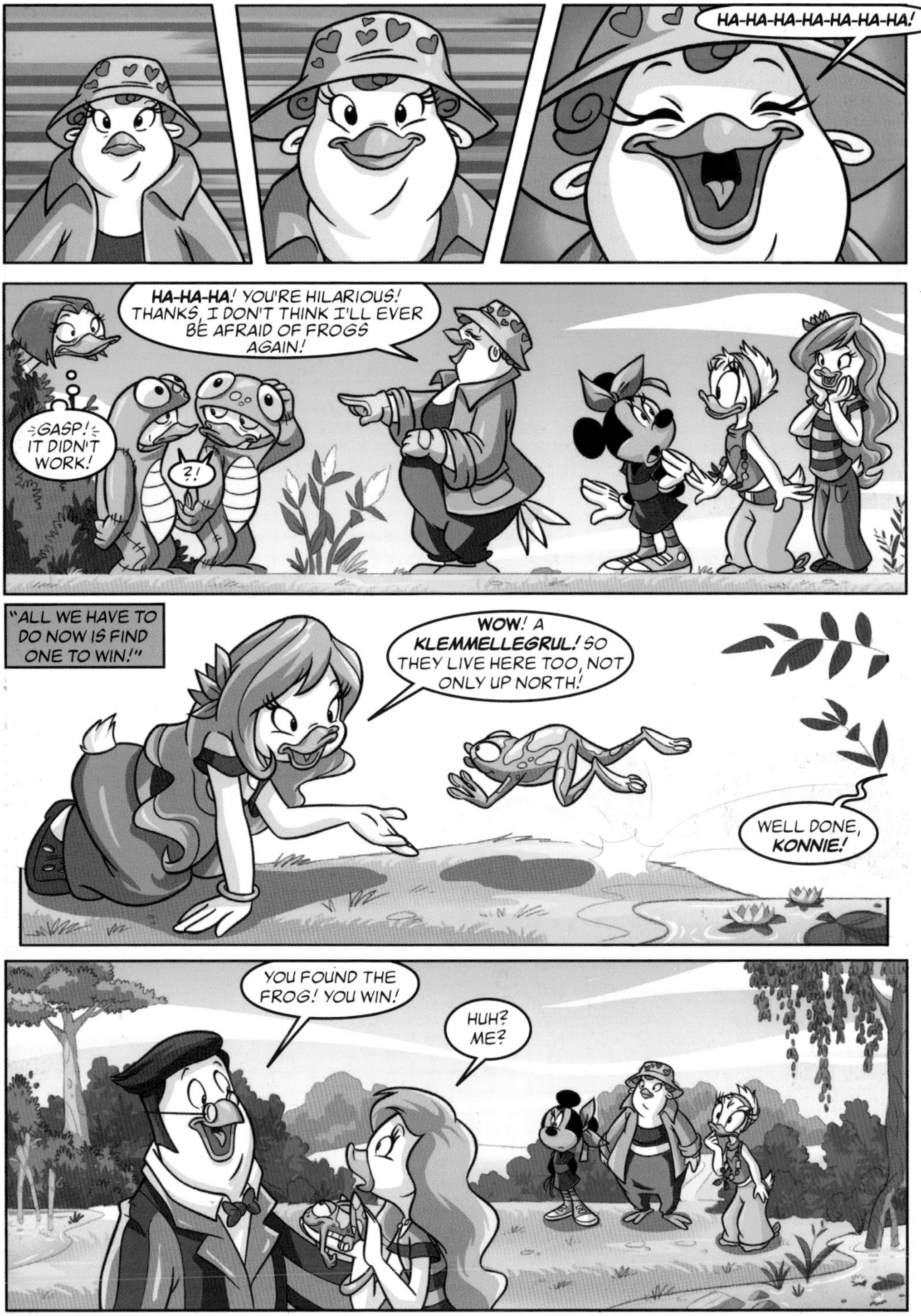
HA-HA-HA-HA-HA-HA-HA!
HA-HA-HA! YOU'RE HILARIOUS! THANKS, I DON'T THINK I'LL EVER BE AFRAID OF FROGS AGAIN!
GASP! IT DIDN'T WORK!
?!
"ALL WE HAVE TO DO NOW IS FIND ONE TO WIN!"
WOW! A KLEMMELLEGRUL! SO THEY LIVE HERE TOO, NOT ONLY UP NORTH!
WELL DONE, KONNIE!
YOU FOUND THE FROG! YOU WIN!
HUH? ME?

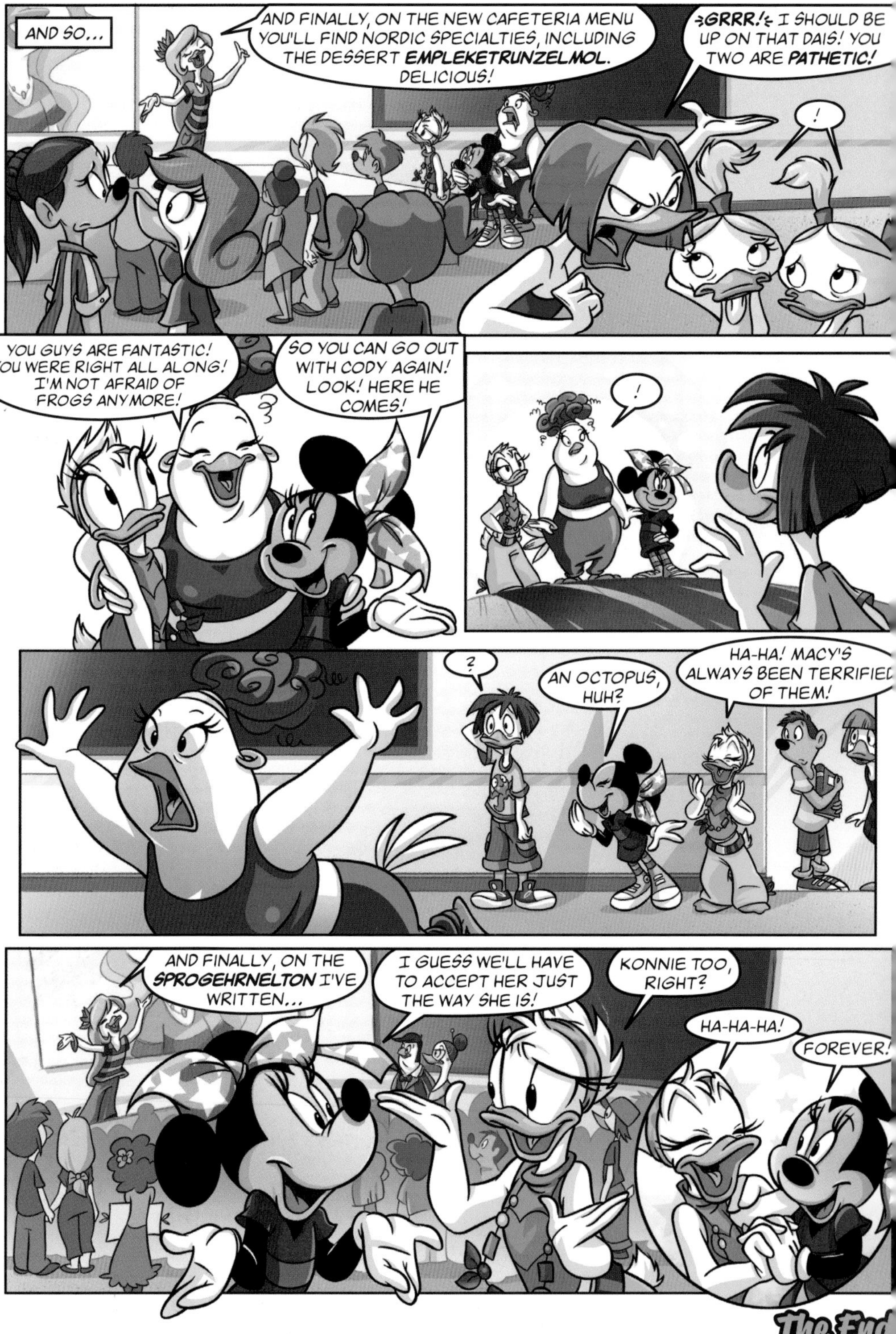
AND SO...
AND FINALLY, ON THE NEW CAFETERIA MENU YOU'LL FIND NORDIC SPECIALTIES, INCLUDING THE DESSERT EMPLEKETRUNZELMOL. DELICIOUS!
GRRR! I SHOULD BE UP ON THAT DAIS! YOU TWO ARE PATHETIC!
!
YOU GUYS ARE FANTASTIC! YOU WERE RIGHT ALL ALONG! I'M NOT AFRAID OF FROGS ANYMORE!
SO YOU CAN GO OUT WITH CODY AGAIN! LOOK! HERE HE COMES!
!
?
AN OCTOPUS, HUH?
HA-HA! MACY'S ALWAYS BEEN TERRIFIE OF THEM!
AND FINALLY, ON THE SPROGEHRNELTON I'VE WRITTEN...
I GUESS WE'LL HAVE TO ACCEPT HER JUST THE WAY SHE IS!
KONNIE TOO, RIGHT?
HA-HA-HA!
FOREVER!
The End

WATCH OUT FOR PAPERCUTZ

Welcome to the sensational sixth DISNEY GRAPHIC NOVEL, or as we prefer to call it, the second, simply-stunning MINNIE & DAISY graphic novel—from Papercutz, those mild-mannered Mouseketeers totally dedicated to publishing great graphic novels for all ages. I'm Jim Salicrup, the Editor-in-Chief and Substitute Leader of the Club That's-Made-for-You-and-Me, and I'm here to talk about mice and ducks and even a blue donkey...

First, there's a really cute mouse called Cheese who has appeared in several DISNEY FAIRIES graphic novels, the most recent being DISNEY FAIRIES #20 "Tinker Bell and a Far-Too-Secret Secret." Cheese is more like the kind of pet mouse you're likely to find in most pet shops, and the fairies of Pixie Hollow simply adore Cheese. If you enjoy the comics in MINNIE & DAISY, I bet you'll love the comics in DISNEY FAIRIES #20, in addition to Cheese, it also features Bobble, Clank, Fairy Mary, Fluffy, Gliss, Iridessa, Lizzie, Rosetta, Silvermist, Terence, Vidia, and oh, yeah, Tinker Bell!

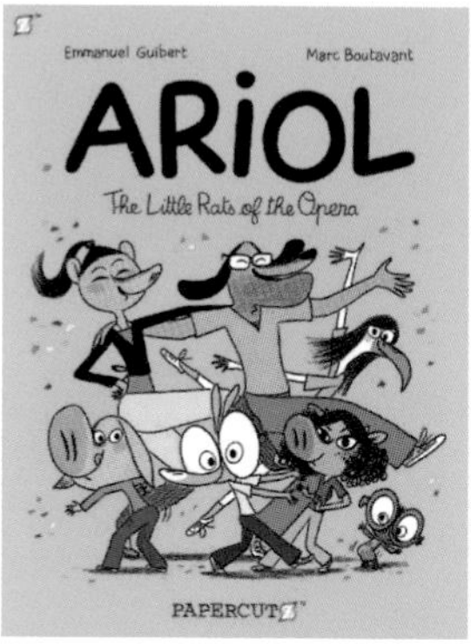
Emmanuel Guibert
Marc Boutavant
ARiOL
The Little Rats of the Opera
PAPERCUTZ

Second, there's a character who's not quite a mouse, but a guy, with superhuman reflexes and intuition, called Rat. He's part of the Maxwell's Vanguard organization, and unfortunately they're the bad guys in the DISNEY THE ZODIAC LEGACY graphic novels. The good guys are lead by Steven Lee, who possesses super strength and reflexes. THE ZODIAC LEGACY is the latest creation of comicbook legend Stan Lee. The power of the Zodiac comes from twelve pools of mystical energy. Due to a sabotaged experiment, twelve magical superpowers are unleashed on Steven Lee and twelve others. If you enjoy tales of teenage super-heroes, you should check out THE ZODIAC LEGACY.

Third, there's perhaps the most famouse, er, I mean famous mouse in the world—and that's Mickey Mouse, and he's been starring in some of his wildest adventures ever! In DISNEY GREAT PARODIES, Mickey stars in a spoof of one of the greatest works of poetry—The Divine Comedy by Durante degli Alighieri, better known as Dante. Minnie Mouse only appears for one page, but it's a cameo appearance that packs quite a wallop—for Mickey! All sorts of other Disney super-stars pop up, including Donald Duck (twice!) in hilarious guest-appearances. Then there's DISNEY X-MICKEY which features Mickey and a strangely familiar fellow called Pipwolf in supernatural adventures. In fact, Mickey originally got drawn into these spooky happenings when he went to a park hoping to find Minnie's lost powder compact in the first X-MICKEY tale, "In The Mirror." If you enjoy MINNIE & DAISY, you might also enjoy Mickey's graphic novels!

Finally, there's another character I wanted to tell you about that I hope you'll like. He's a blue donkey, his best friend is a pig, and he's in love with a cow. He's ARIOL, and we have a special preview of ARIOL #10 "Little Rats of the Opera," (which actually aren't rats, but dance students) on the following pages. Written by Emmanuel Guibert and drawn by Marc Boutavant, ARIOL is an award-winning graphic novel series that appeals to everyone who has ever been a kid! We hope you enjoy it!

Despite how different all of these graphic novels may appear to you at first, there's something they all have in common with MINNIE & DAISY (besides mice, rats, or ducks), and that's friendship. Whether they're flitting about spreading pixie dust or battling villains as a team of Zodiac-powered heroes or exploring supernatural worlds or just have a passion for fashion, all of these wonderful characters know the importance of true friendship. So no matter how much trouble there may be in the world at any given moment, just remember, if ducks, mice, blue donkeys, and pigs can all get along—then there's hope for us too!

Jim

STAY IN TOUCH!

EMAIL:	salicrup@papercutz.com
WEB:	www.papercutz.com
TWITTER:	@papercutzgn
INSTAGRAM	@papercutzgn
FACEBOOK:	PAPERCUTZGRAPHICNOVELS
REGULAR MAIL:	Papercutz, 160 Broadway, Suite 700, East Wing, New York, NY 10038

Special Preview of ARIOL #10 "Little Rats of the Opera"

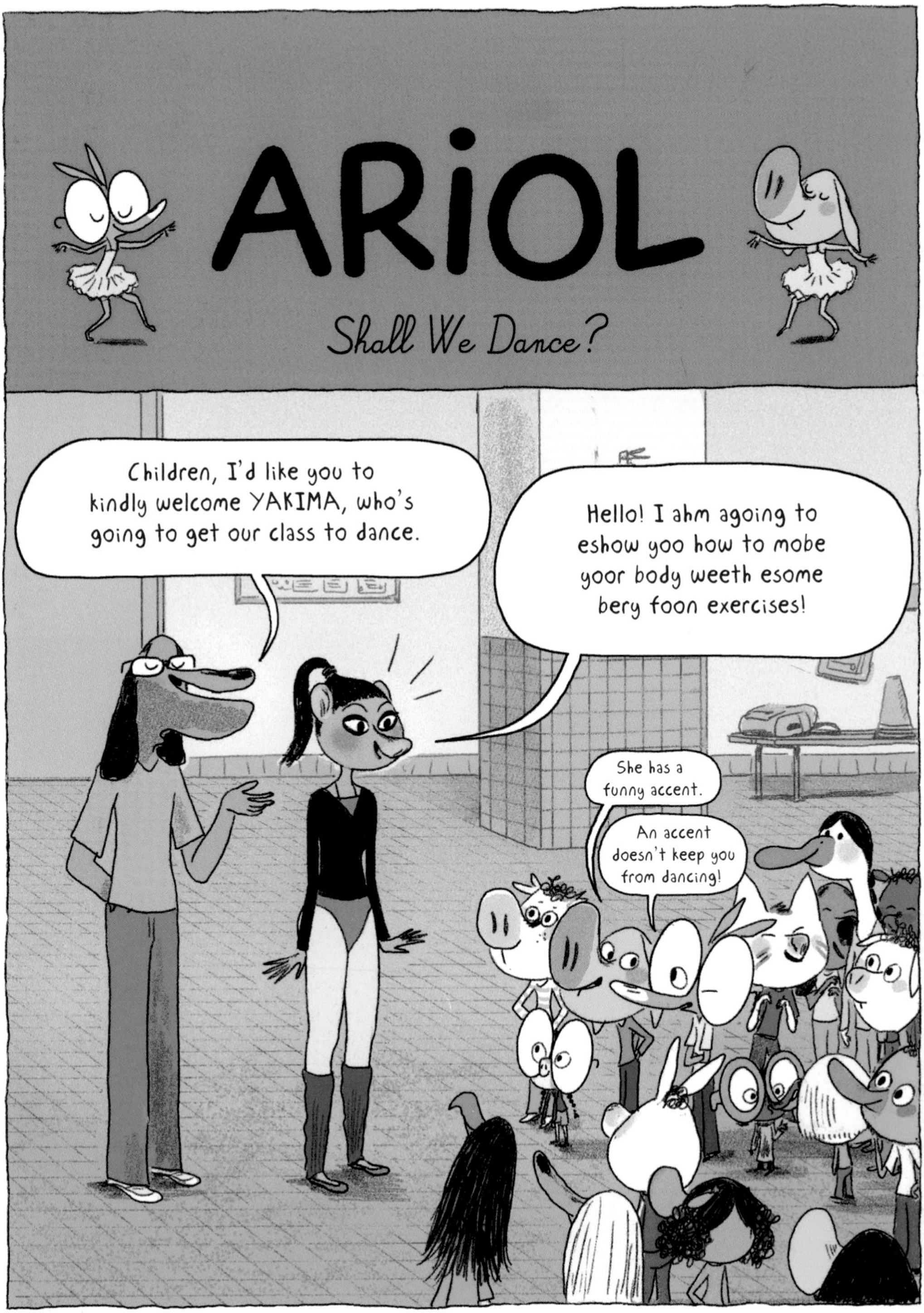
ARiOL
Shall We Dance?
Children, I'd like you to kindly welcome YAKIMA, who's going to get our class to dance.
Hello! I ahm agoing to eshow yoo how to mobe yoor body weeth esome bery foon exercises!
She has a funny accent.
An accent doesn't keep you from dancing!

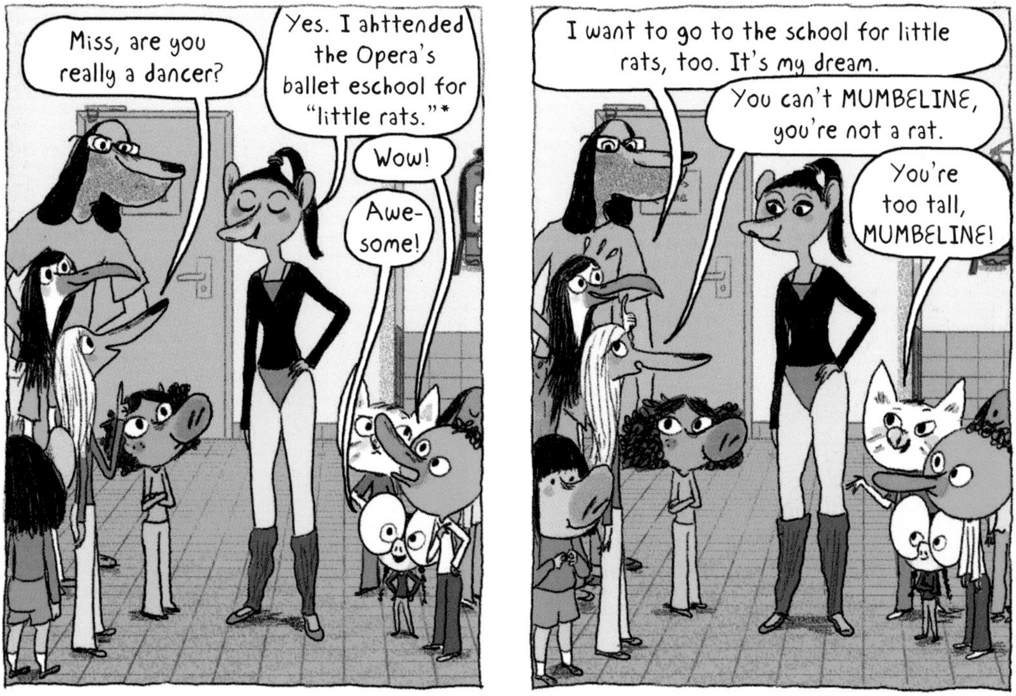
Miss, are you really a dancer?
Yes. I ahttended the Opera's ballet eschool for "little rats."*
Wow!
Awe-some!
I want to go to the school for little rats, too. It's my dream.
You can't MUMBELINE, you're not a rat.
You're too tall, MUMBELINE!

*In France, the student dancers at the Paris Opera are called "little rats."

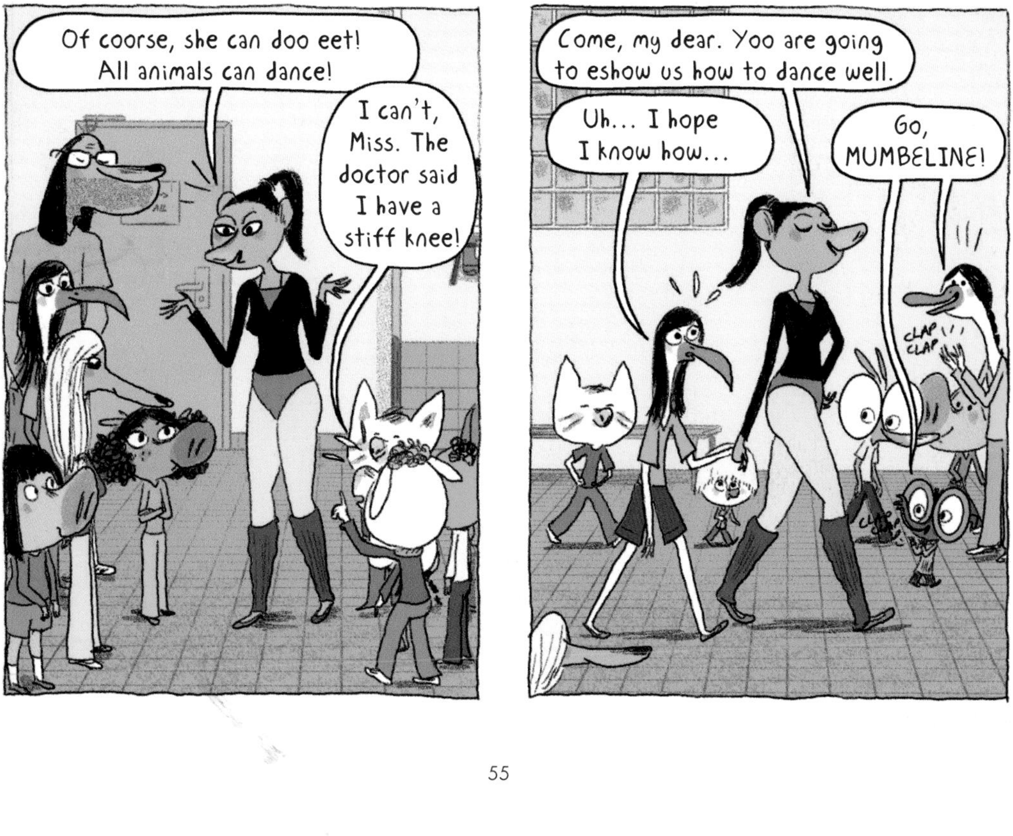
Of coorse, she can doo eet! All animals can dance!
I can't, Miss. The doctor said I have a stiff knee!
Come, my dear. Yoo are going to eshow us how to dance well.
Uh... I hope I know how...
Go, MUMBELINE!
CLAP CLAP

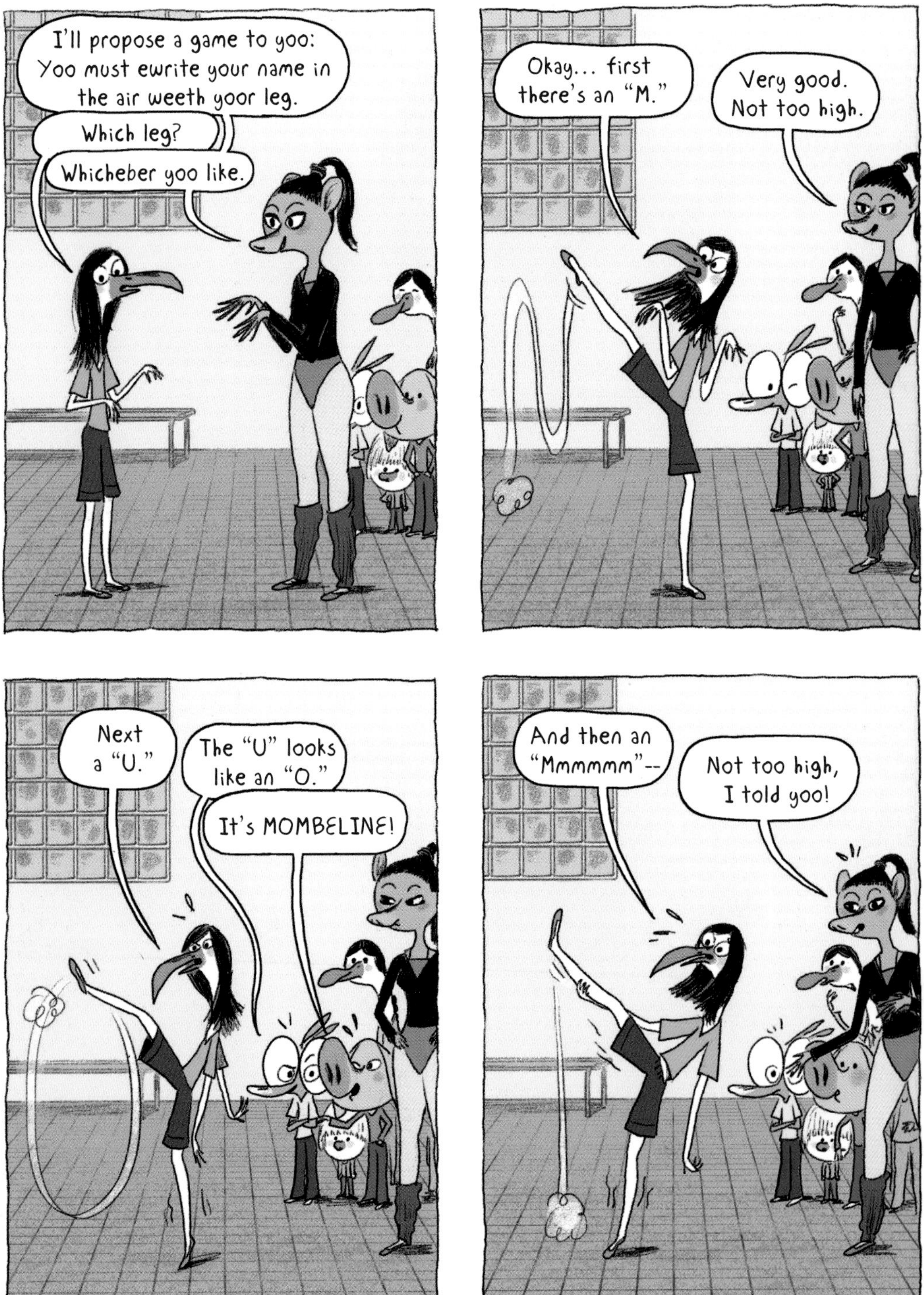
I'll propose a game to yoo: Yoo must ewrite your name in the air weeth yoor leg.
Which leg?
Whicheber yoo like.
Okay... first there's an "M."
Very good. Not too high.
Next a "U."
The "U" looks like an "O."
It's MOMBELINE!
And then an "Mmmmmm"--
Not too high, I told yoo!

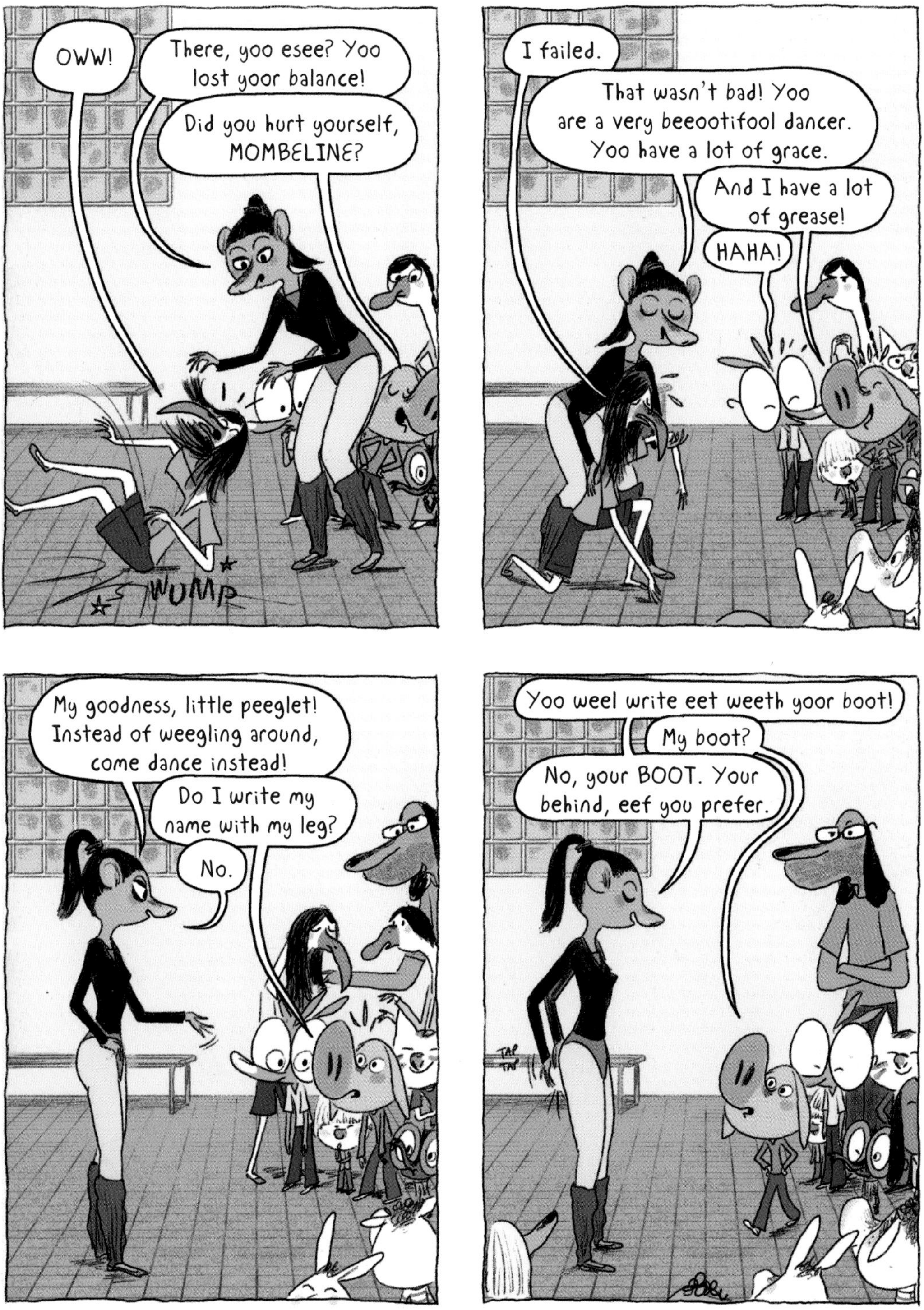
OWW!
There, yoo esee? Yoo lost yoor balance!
Did you hurt yourself, MOMBELINE?
WUMP
I failed.
That wasn't bad! Yoo are a very beeootifool dancer. Yoo have a lot of grace.
And I have a lot of grease!
HAHA!
My goodness, little peeglet! Instead of weegling around, come dance instead!
Do I write my name with my leg?
No.
Yoo weel write eet weeth yoor boot!
My boot?
No, your BOOT. Your behind, eef you prefer.
TAP TAP

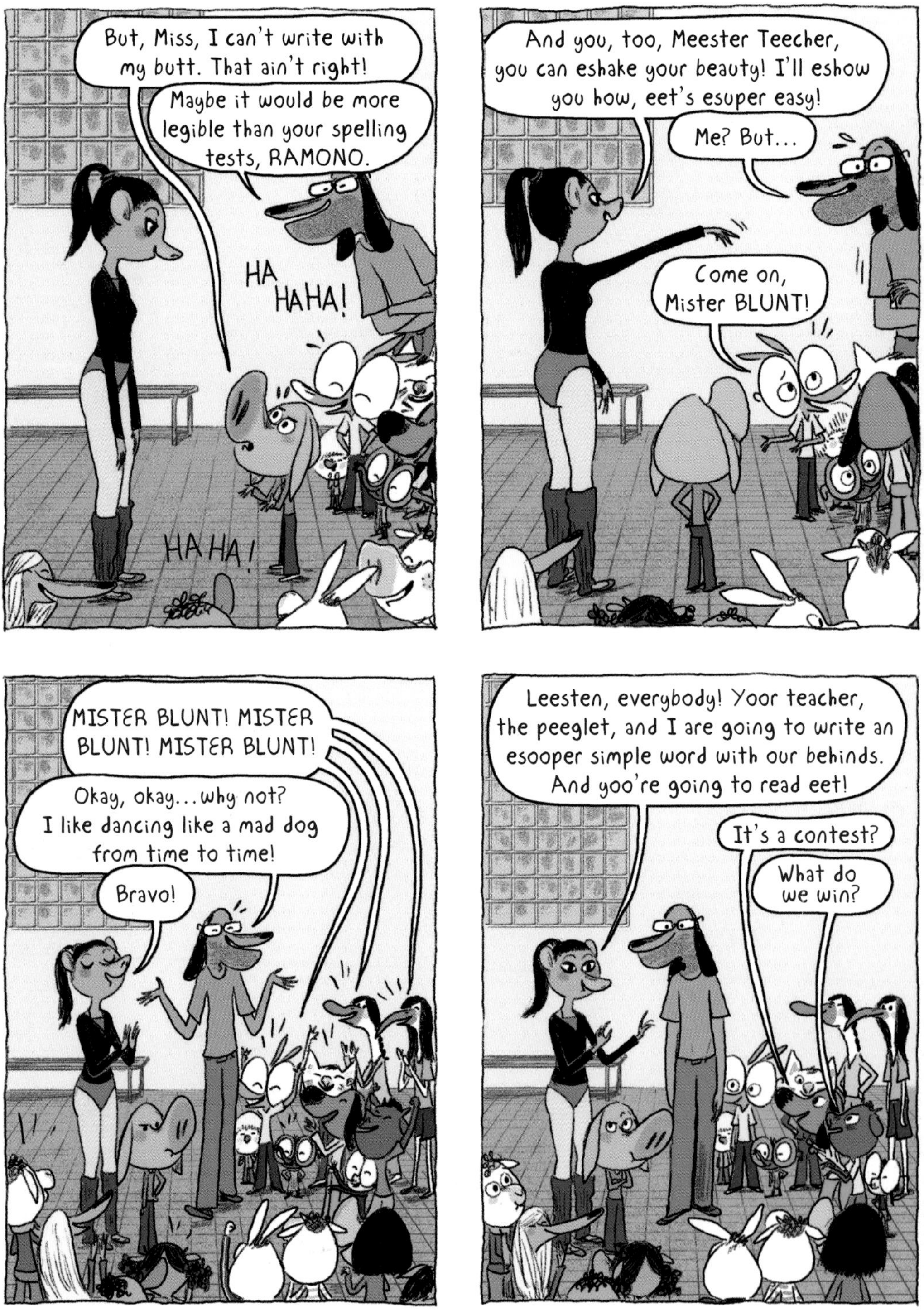

But, Miss, I can't write with my butt. That ain't right!
Maybe it would be more legible than your spelling tests, RAMONO.
HA HAHA!
HA HA!
And you, too, Meester Teecher, you can eshake your beauty! I'll eshow you how, eet's esuper easy!
Me? But...
Come on, Mister BLUNT!
MISTER BLUNT! MISTER BLUNT! MISTER BLUNT!
Okay, okay...why not? I like dancing like a mad dog from time to time!
Bravo!
Leesten, everybody! Yoor teacher, the peeglet, and I are going to write an esooper simple word with our behinds. And yoo're going to read eet!
It's a contest?
What do we win?

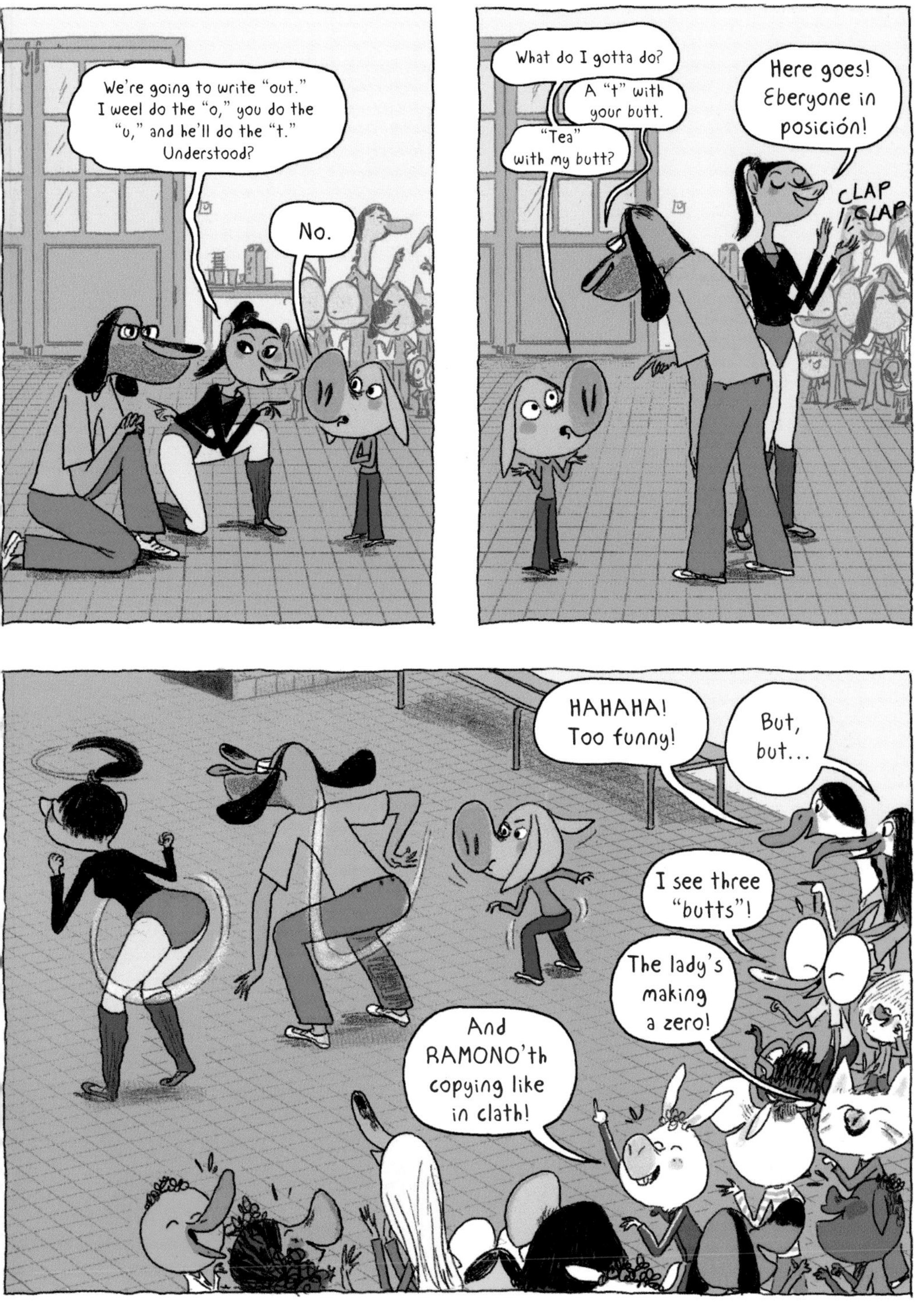
We're going to write "out." I weel do the "o," you do the "u," and he'll do the "t." Understood?
No.
What do I gotta do?
A "t" with your butt.
"Tea" with my butt?
Here goes! Eberyone in posición!
CLAP CLAP
HAHAHA! Too funny!
But, but...
I see three "butts"!
The lady's making a zero!
And RAMONO'th copying like in clath!

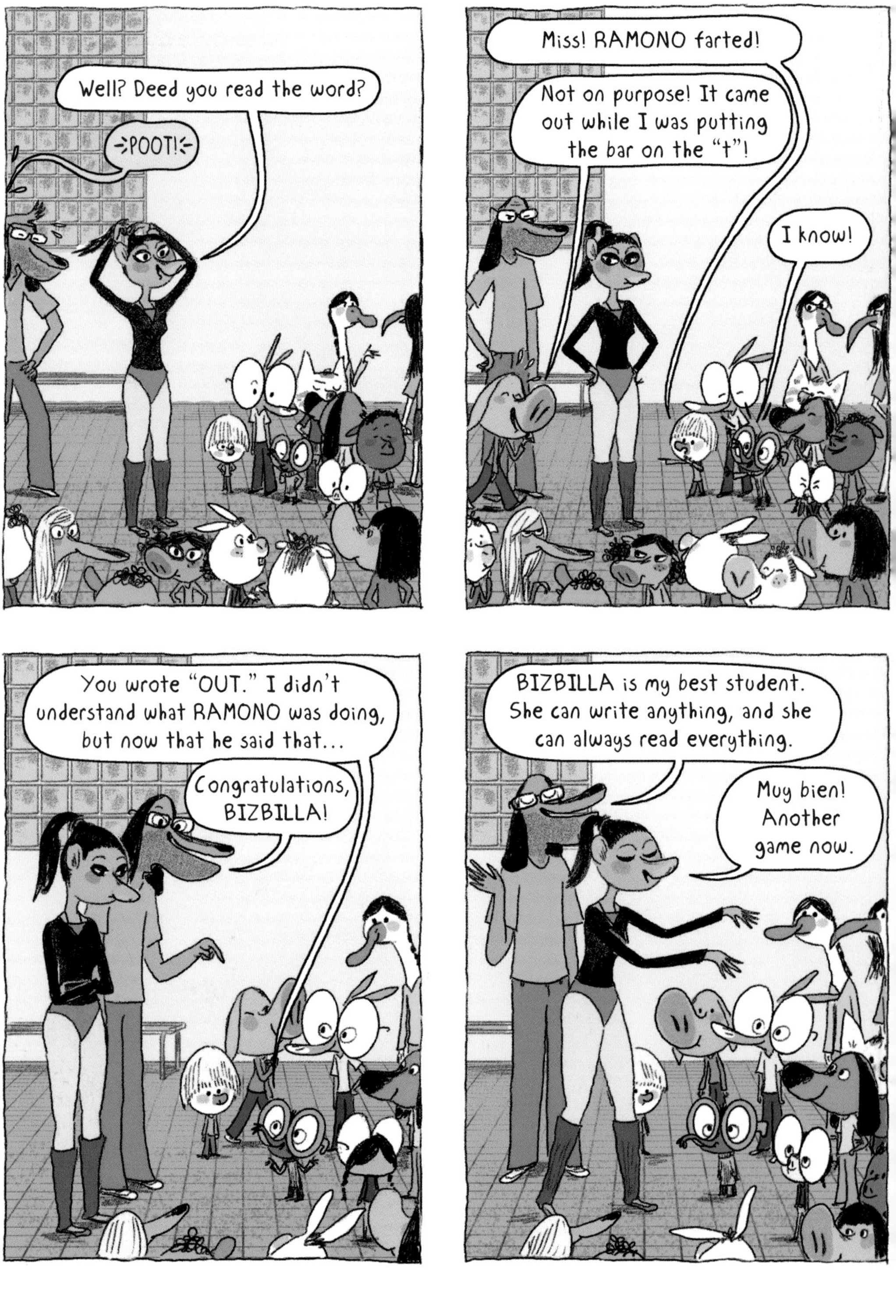
Well? Deed you read the word?
POOT!
Miss! RAMONO farted!
Not on purpose! It came out while I was putting the bar on the "t"!
I know!
You wrote "OUT." I didn't understand what RAMONO was doing, but now that he said that...
Congratulations, BIZBILLA!
BIZBILLA is my best student. She can write anything, and she can always read everything.
Muy bien! Another game now.

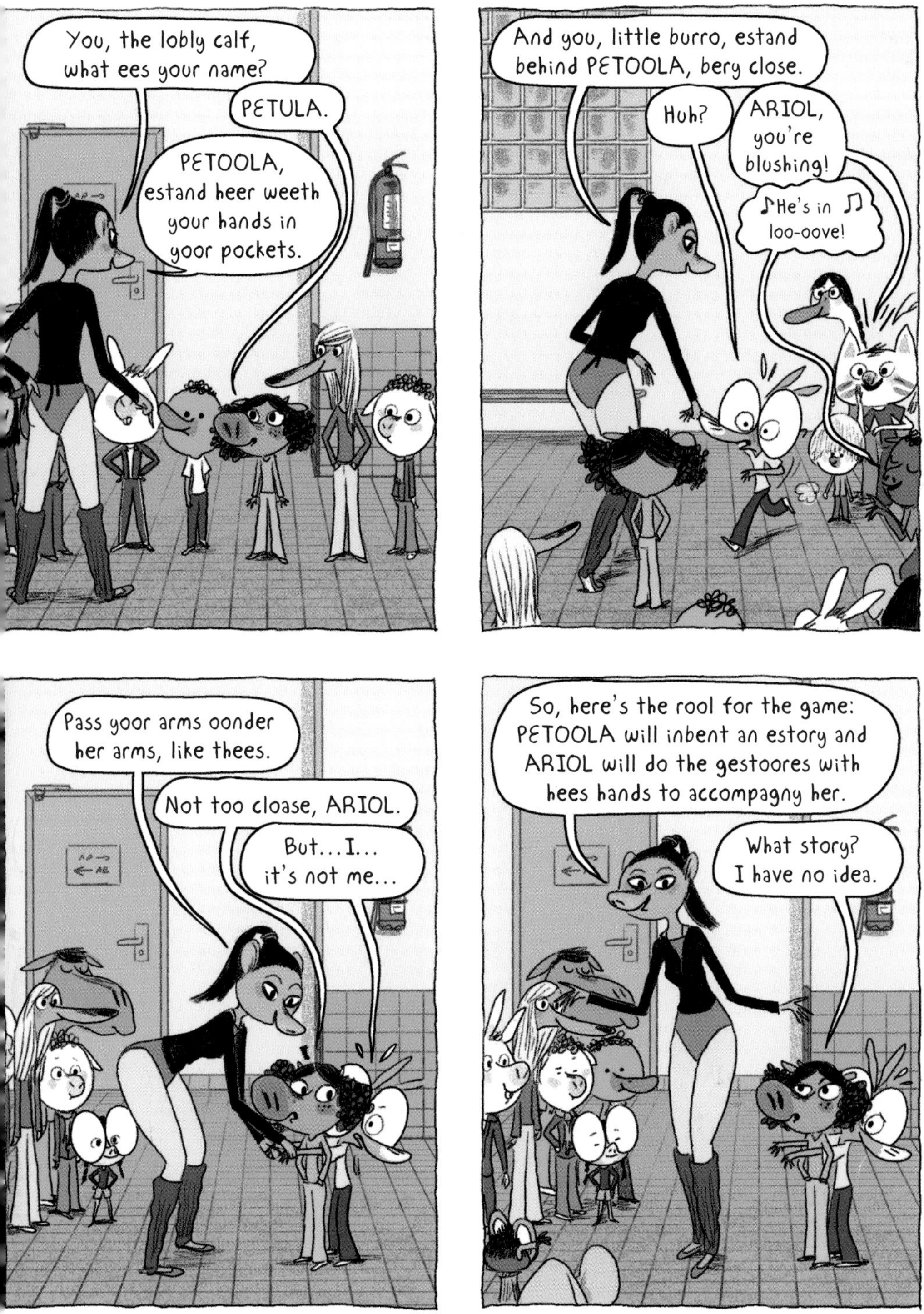
You, the lobly calf, what ees your name?
PETULA.
PETOOLA, estand heer weeth your hands in yoor pockets.
And you, little burro, estand behind PETOOLA, bery close.
Huh?
ARIOL, you're blushing!
♪He's in ♫ loo-oove!
Pass yoor arms oonder her arms, like thees.
Not too cloase, ARIOL.
But... I... it's not me...
So, here's the rool for the game: PETOOLA will inbent an estory and ARIOL will do the gestoores with hees hands to accompagny her.
What story? I have no idea.

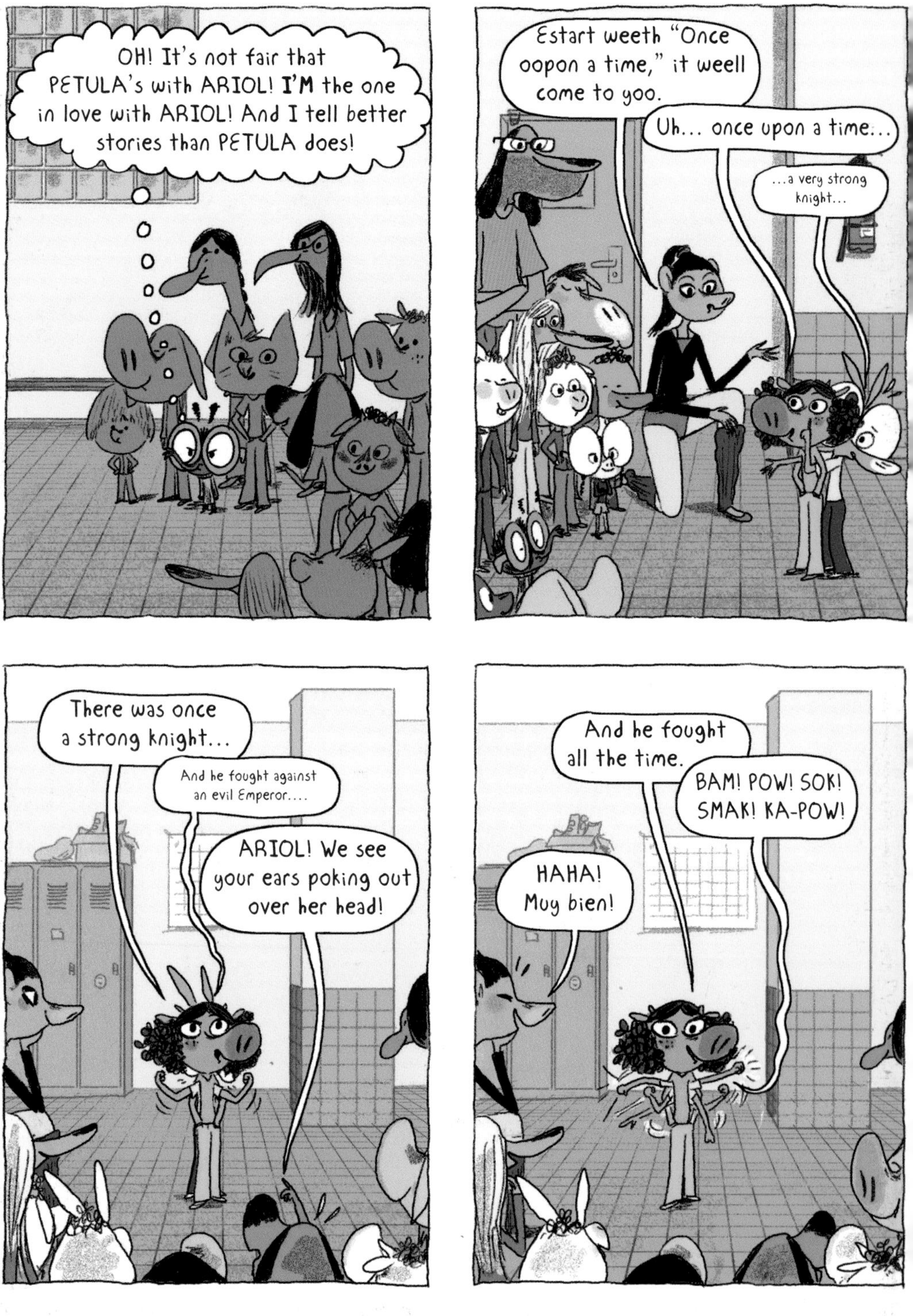

OH! It's not fair that PETULA's with ARIOL! **I'M** the one in love with ARIOL! And I tell better stories than PETULA does!
Estart weeth "Once oopon a time," it weell come to yoo.
Uh... once upon a time...
...a very strong knight...
There was once a strong knight...
And he fought against an evil Emperor....
ARIOL! We see your ears poking out over her head!
And he fought all the time.
BAM! POW! SOK! SMAK! KA-POW!
HAHA! Muy bien!

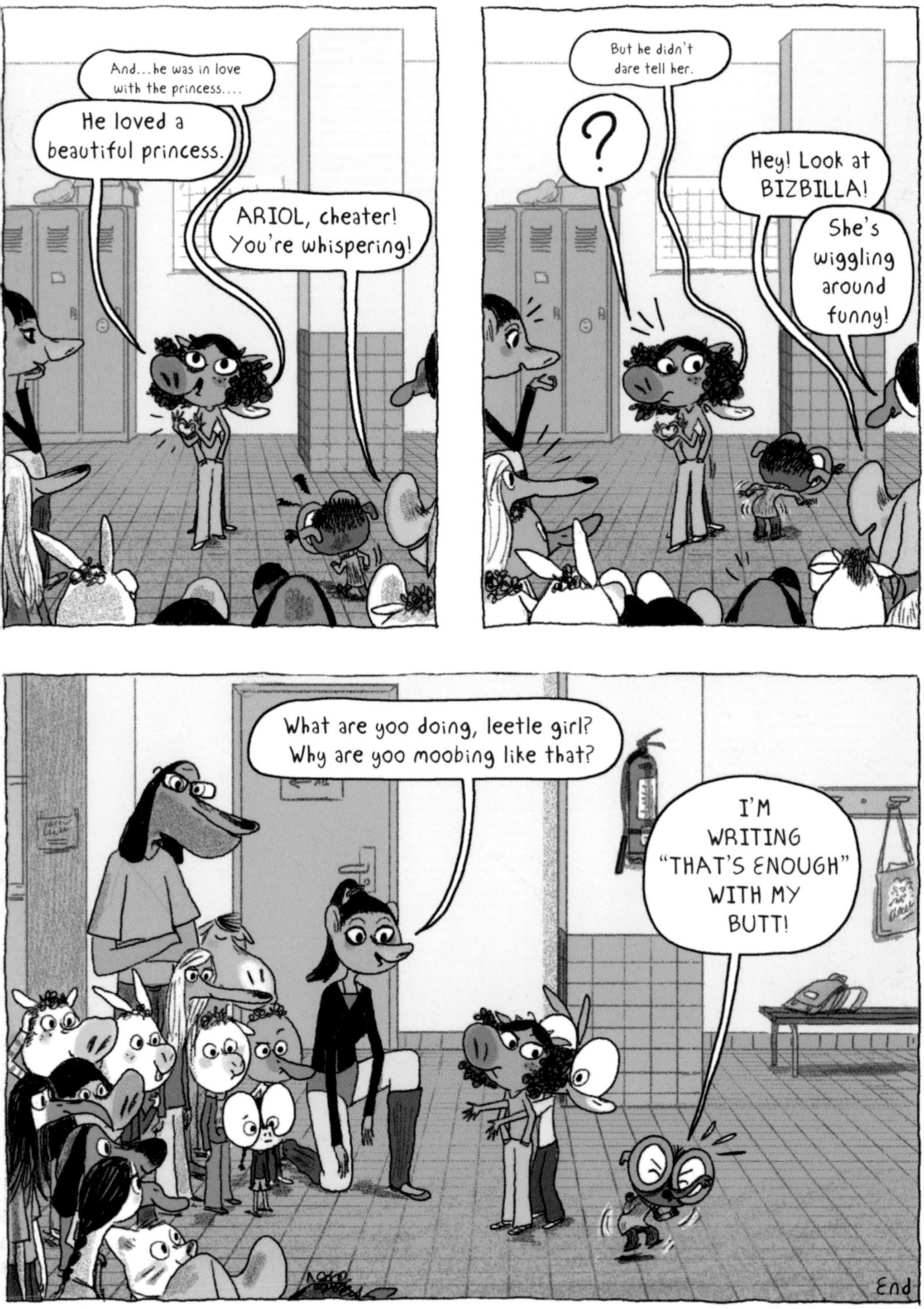

And...he was in love with the princess....
He loved a beautiful princess.
ARIOL, cheater! You're whispering!
But he didn't dare tell her.
?
Hey! Look at BIZBILLA!
She's wiggling around funny!
What are yoo doing, leetle girl? Why are yoo moobing like that?
I'M WRITING "THAT'S ENOUGH" WITH MY BUTT!
End

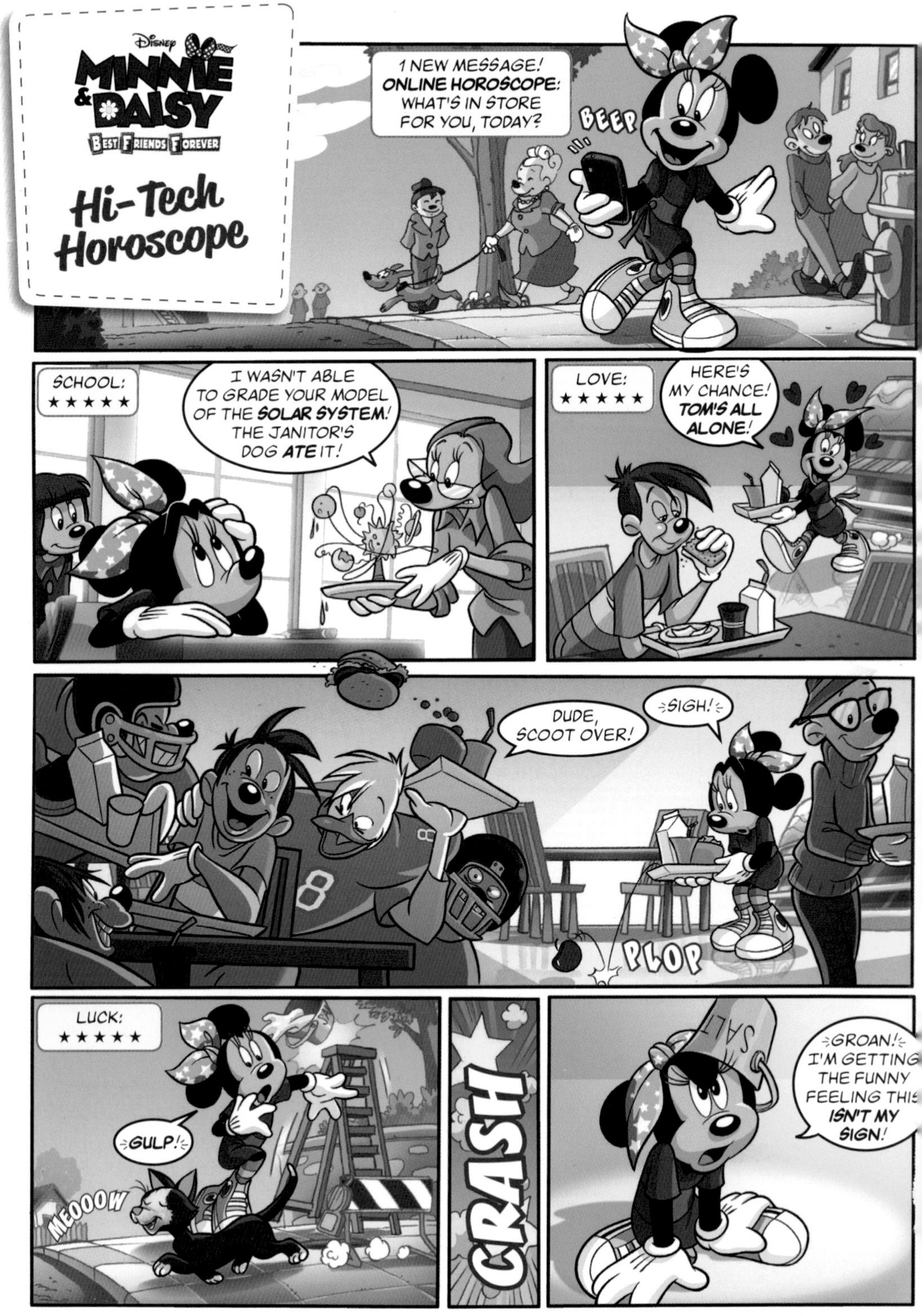
Disney
MINNIE & DAISY
BEST FRIENDS FOREVER
Hi-Tech Horoscope
1 NEW MESSAGE! ONLINE HOROSCOPE: WHAT'S IN STORE FOR YOU, TODAY?
BEEP
SCHOOL: ★★★★★
I WASN'T ABLE TO GRADE YOUR MODEL OF THE SOLAR SYSTEM! THE JANITOR'S DOG ATE IT!
LOVE: ★★★★★
HERE'S MY CHANCE! TOM'S ALL ALONE!
DUDE, SCOOT OVER!
SIGH!
PLOP
LUCK: ★★★★★
GULP!
MEOOOW
CRASH
GROAN! I'M GETTING THE FUNNY FEELING THIS ISN'T MY SIGN!
The End